RIZE KEER

FIGHTING THE CURRENT

BOOK 2 IN THE SERIES

L.M. FILI

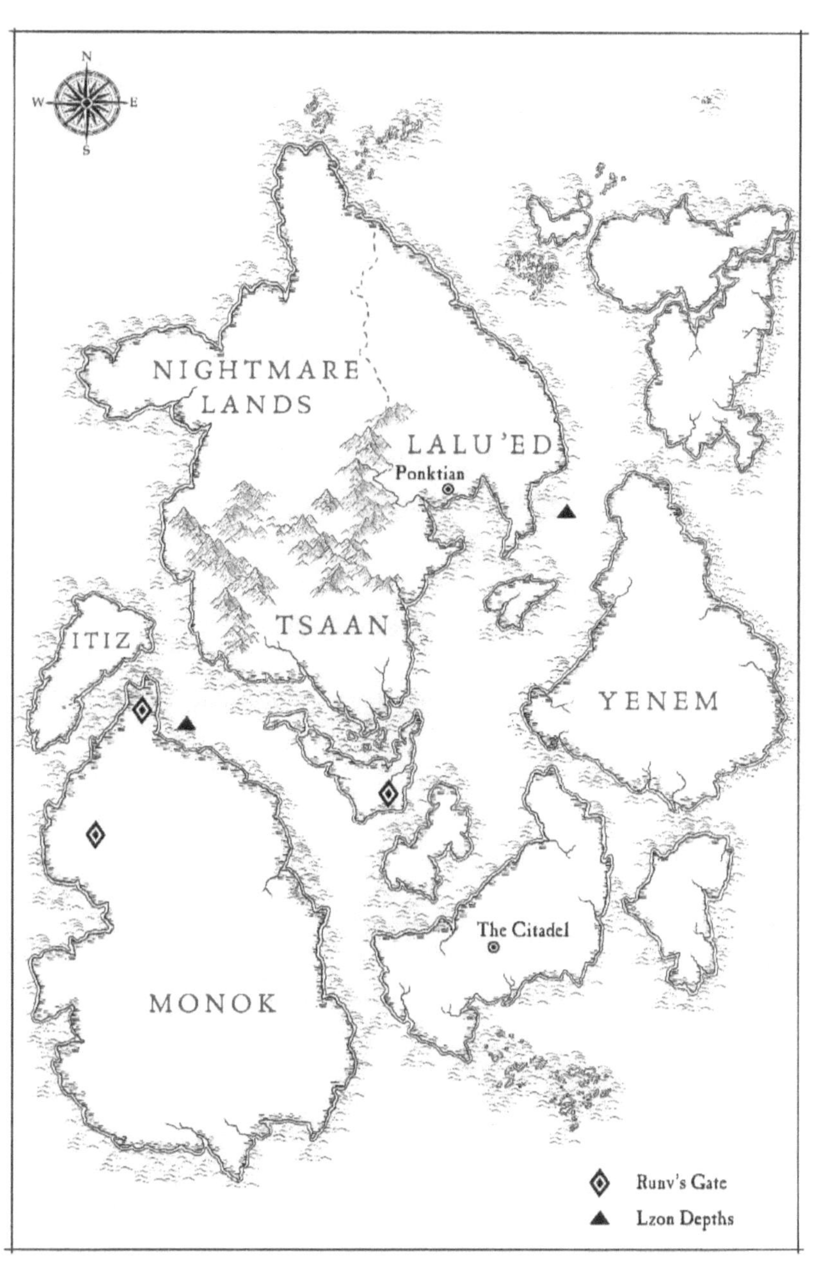

N
W E
S
NIGHTMARE
LANDS
LALU'ED
Ponktian
TSAAN
ITIZ
YENEM
MONOK
The Citadel
Runv's Gate
Lzon Depths

To Trevor and all people who think that masking
and people pleasing is a good idea.

Kindness without honesty is manipulation.
Honesty without kindness is cruelty.

Enjoy the reading and let it shape your spirit.

Contents

Characters from Book One

- Rize Keer. A mentor from Lalu'Ed. Has problems with her magic and critical thinking.
- Amethyst. A telepathic Worock wildcat. Too smart to be bothered.
- Rel. The Great One's advisor, a trained custodian. Wears a hood.
- Grant. A trained custodian. Works with Worock cats. Rel's friend.
- Eal Coras. The Great One.
- Mar'Anna. The Empress of Tsaan.
- The Ladies in White. A forbidden cult. Serve as the empress's seers.
- The Dolmen of Attraction. Performs miracles beyond our imagination.
- Koryn. A demon. Guards the Dolmen and is sick of it.
- Liara Ent. The Great One from the times before. Rebelled against the Citadel's order. Started a war.
- The Elders. Observe the Great One's decisions. Protect the Citadel order.

Before all elements, beware of the water.

As a shapeshifter dissolves his kind face into monstrous,
so the water brings death to the weak and shallow-hearted.

Those who have been claimed by fire are doomed
and can never return to the infernal kingdom.

Thus, the water keens to cleanse the flame-touch
to mark us with wounds that hurt deeper.

Blessed be the challenge circle that is crawling with dread.

I am the fire. I am the water. I am the brass.

— Chant of Challenge 2:1

Prologue
Rel

"Your Excellency, it'd be foolish of me to convey such a thing, but…"

Rel chose his words carefully. He was a cautious man — too experienced to gift servants a chance to eavesdrop. He drilled the front door with a stare.

I definitely heard something. A creak?

"Spit it out before you burst," Eal Coras cheered up his advisor.

Rel ignored him. One of the few pleasures he was allowed to have within these walls. His ears burning, his body tensed and stressed, he tried to detect an intruder if there was one.

Nothing.

The silence lingered in the Great One's office, soundlessly singing for human ears in its crystal voice. Now, Rel heard it clearly. Hungry and demanding to catch the subtlest whisper, it witnessed two men making history.

"If the Elders' spies infiltrated this room, I would've noticed." Eal lost his patience.

"So, you knew we were alone for sure." A sigh escaped his chest. Rel took off his hood, and a sudden pain pierced his eyes. Getting used to the light, he gave Eal an annoyed look. "You *made* me speak formally."

"For the sake of practice," Eal said, clearly enjoying Rel's frustration. "Your diplomacy will be needed soon."

"You sound pompously cryptic. Makes me nauseous." Rel rubbed his eyes, stepping away from the irritating sunlight.

The Great One said nothing but watched his advisor closely. Plunged into their own thoughts, they enjoyed the peace while it lasted.

The summer turned out to be charming with its loving sun, warm days, and diamond nights. Everyone would've embraced the marvellous view from the windows that overlooked Academy Town, but not Rel. He was sick of the place which made him almost fly to the Citadel when Eal requested a meeting. Finally, the big man would give him and his squad a job.

"So?" Rel lifted his eyebrow. "Would you grant the Geckos an op or am I here for another round of *'I need you to stay here'*?"

Eal hesitated, pursing his lips. He opened his mouth but shut it shortly. He was stalling on purpose. A glimpse of fear reflected in his eyes as if voicing the truth would banish him to the darkest dimension full of carnivorous monsters.

"I've lost the Bone," he finally uttered.

"Don't you think it's a healer's problem?" Rel snorted, though Eal ignored his mockery. "Wait. Do you mean *the* Bone? THE BONE?!"

"Stop wailing like a professional mourner," Eal hissed. Grabbing Rel's collar sharply, he shook the man. "Be quiet."

"Was it stolen?" Rel wheezed, fighting the grip. The Great One nodded. "When?"

"One week before the Blossom Feast," Eal said, and left his advisor standing in sheer disbelief. "Should've told you right away, but—"

"There's plenty of things you should've done," Rel spat his poison. "But this? This is the next level of absurd!"

They argued as the last amber ray of sunset gave its farewell. It caressed the Great One's bearded check, ignited the golden threads of his attire, then slid below the horizon. Dark and eerie, the room's ambience seemed like a perfect harbour for a shameful secret.

"No, Rel. It's too dangerous, Rel," he mimicked Eal's voice, giving it an extra hoarseness. "You don't have the clearance for that. Just escort me. Is it so hard to follow the order?"

The Great One watched the unravelling scene, his mouth open.

"I can hardly remember if you've played the performance card in our fights before. You spend too much time with that girl, Rel." Eal's lips pursed in disgust. "Please, spare me. Let's speak like adults."

"We'll discuss Rize, be sure of that. But now!" Rel fumed. "Are you telling me that we travelled to Lalu'Ed to get back the most dangerous magical artefact in our collection—" he panted and shook his head, refusing to believe his ears, "—and your cover was a stupid greenhorn recruitment?!"

"And lovemaking festival," Eal shrugged. "Always liked the Lalu'Edian version. So rural, so…wild."

Rel stood dumbfounded, afraid to blink. "My jaw just landed in the Runv civilisation."

"That's deep."

"Can't say if you were seriously brainless or brainlessly serious it would work. Either way it's appalling," he said, seeing Eal's smirk. "No wonder the city burned to ashes. The mission was planned by a bunch of elderly idiots! I have the most talented people under my command! Laily can sneak to unsneakable places. Crypt opens anything that has a door. Bram is worth more than a dozen soldiers. Chour could put the whole Citadel to sleep if I let him—"

"You're forgetting the lady Angenia. She is a divine blessing to your team."

"I know about your affairs," Rel retorted. "Stop teasing her with a position by your side. She's mine! And you… you…" He roared unable to speak his mind.

The Great One rolled his eyes, waiting for Rel's tantrum to end. "I'll tell Elder Air you judged his genius plan."

"If he's still in the Citadel, don't bother. I'll do it myself," Rel grunted.

"Wait till the morning," Eal said. "You know how sensitive he is towards his day schedule, and you…" — he shrugged — "you're not in a good shape right now."

Taking a deep breath, Rel closed his eyes as anger threatened to overwhelm the last drops of clear thinking he had saved. He needed a cool head. After all, isn't that what he taught Rize these weeks past? He knew who he was. How murderous he could become if his magic goes rogue. *That girl* could stun people accidentally while Rel was able to wipe out entire cities.

Control ruled his body and mind, making it impossible to know the real Rel. Frankly, he failed to know himself. It'd been years since he ran away to reach his true nature, but the only thing he discovered was fear. He was a coward, avoidant and delicate — the combination of traits that always ruined lives. Coming back to the Elders was the right call, even though he hated it.

Nothing could make his life better or safer for others but cold-hearted authority over what made Rel a person. He was the second Great One — an anomaly that deserved to be hidden away for the sake of others. He had no right to have an identity. He was a function.

"Is that why you need my diplomacy?" Rel uttered, rubbing his sign of Greatness as if it could be cleaned off his forehead. "Am I going to the Runv civilisation?"

"You can send someone from your squad if that girl—"

"Rize," he stressed.

Eal pursed his lips patiently. "If *Rize* requires your full attention. The Elders and I need to know the Runvish reports are not forged."

A plan started to brew in Rel's head. He could fix this. He knew he would if Eal agreed to provide him with all the information.

"If someone knows about the artefact," he thought aloud, "they've stolen it to bring Liara back to life. Her blood is still in Runv's royal treasury, I hope."

"For now," the Great One nodded. "Only fanatics know about this possibility. Do you see now how wet and fishy it is?"

"Stingray," Rel spat, and chills ran down his spine. "His men stole Liara's Bone… Huh." Rel smirked at the coincidence. "I saw some burnt bodies at the Blossom Feast. They had the stingray embroidery on their armour." He took a shallow breath, his heart shrinking with a pang. "The old man must be behind it."

"Everything points to that," Eal agreed. "That's one more reason why I want *you* to do it. You've met. Maybe he's not beyond reason and just wants something."

The last thing Rel needed was to meet the man who played and abused his cowardice first-hand. Even thoughts of that brought chilling memories of what Stingray made him do.

Distant screams.

Rel buried that part of his life and ran back to the Citadel like a child. Though he was nothing but a teenage boy back then, he couldn't shake off the shame to this day.

"Make him talk," the man's tender voice reached Rel's memories as the echoes of screams became louder.

Frowning, Rel silenced his past with a heavy heart. He wanted to find an excuse to reject Eal's task, though none justified it. Except, maybe, animal fear, but he'd better die before admitting that to the Great One.

"How secure is the Runv civilisation now?" Rel asked instead.

"I get their reports monthly, as usual. No new mercenaries. No accidents in the tunnels," Eal seemed concerned. "Even the underground king seemed less sarcastic last time we spoke."

"Poor symptom to detect his insanity."

"Therefore, he's in good health."

"Which means…" Rel crossed his arms, still recovering from the memories that stormed his mind. "The blood diamond hasn't woken yet. That's good. If we're lucky, my team could extract the diamond from the Runvish treasury and destroy the temple in one week."

"Too obvious," Eal shook his head. "You've probably forgotten but the temple is underwater. If Stingray *is* behind this, we won't even cross the Lzon border from there."

Pacing the floor, Rel thought of better options. The more he spoke, the more gibberish his speech became.

"I could ask Chour to dry out the diamond and then Angie would burn the retrieved blood in holy flames."

"Rituals take too long," Eal protested again. "If the gem activates near them, your squad will lose both healers."

"Then, Bram could smash it."

"Doubt that. Liara's blood is infused with dark magic. I'm sure the stone is indestructible."

"Demon!" Rel cursed. "Whilst criticizing, add your point! How are you planning to stop this? If they resurrect Liara, we're finished. Especially you!"

"You're a bad advisor, you know that?"

Eal watched patiently as Rel tried to catch his breath.

"What's your plan?" he asked again.

"Let me think… There'll be three Great Ones who will start an epic war until the world ends," Eal said, playing on Rel's nerves.

He crossed his arms, waiting for a reaction but there was none. "So? Are you done panicking?"

"More or less."

Rel closed his eyes as a sudden pinch of pain crossed his temples. It'd been a while since he had migraines. Them coming back meant little pleasure and much more time with healers.

"See? That's why we stopped telling you anything. You lose your head the moment something goes sideways," Eal said, his voice full of judgment. "I'll brew the herbs."

The Great One opened a side cabinet, tapping impatiently at the golden monogram which spread across its small doors.

It was dark, but Rel knew this room as his own. Tired of arguing, he looked around and cringed at all the gold Eal possessed in his office. Everything screamed of untasteful wealth, starting with peculiar curvy, gold patterns encrusted into oak furniture and ending with numerous shiny, naked figurines of men and women all over the shelves. Some seemed more polished than others, though Rel stopped himself thinking about it too much.

"I must be so special if the Great One himself is cooing over me like a mama-dove," Rel muttered watching as Eal's magic brought a tiny pot of water into bubbles. "You're still keeping this tea-set for me?"

"As we can see, I was right to leave it in my office," Eal said, mixing herbs. "We grew up here together. Studied and trained back-to-back. I'll always treat you as my impudent brother."

"You've got the manners, I've got brains. We're even," Rel grunted and accepted a hot cup with a short hiss as his fingertips scalded. "I need to train Rize in the morning, so…" he took a sip of a healing blend and winced.

Overwhelmed by its bitter aftertaste, Rel failed to utter more sounds.

"That's not important," Eal tilted his head, worried. "You've stopped taking the medicine we gave you, haven't you?"

The ringing silence came back, screwing its way into their ears. Rel sat still with a bored look on his face. Hoping to dodge this topic, he took another sip that turned into an ear-screeching slurp.

"I need you to be well-rested and healthy."

"Send me over to a vacation, then!" Rel put aside his half-finished cup as if it offended him. "Back to business and save our time, please."

Eal's jaw clenched. Clearly his patience was running out as well.

"I have no idea how the bone was snatched from the vault," Eal confessed. "It was secured and guarded. Neither magic nor cryptic wards possessed marks of a robbery. Nothing. It's almost like—"

"Someone transferred Liara's Bone from under the lock." Rel suggested. "There's only one kind of power that is feral enough to do it."

"Now you see why we need the Dolmen's magic?"

"No. I still think it's a foul idea." Rel shrugged. "But if you want to ask its Guardian whether someone used its power, I can send Rize over. She befriended that demon."

"You're joking," Eal said, his eyes widened.

"Do you see a hint of a smile on my face?" Rel crossed his arms, annoyed. "That's why I'm training that idiot three times harder. She could be possessed any time now. I don't know, maybe she's already possessed!"

"Looks like you found yourself a perfect toy for your issues. It explains why you're dragging her around everywhere like a control freak."

"It's your fault," Rel said full of bile. "If you have told me about the Ponktian operation, I wouldn't even let you bring her along. *You* decided to invite her to the Academy."

"That was harsh of me." Eal sighed. "She'll burn anyway, no matter how hard you train her. Your dreams never lie."

"Let's hope she's a phoenix, then," Rel grunted and left the room.

Chapter 1
CHOUR

In the silver moonlight which gently caressed the waving trees behind the window of a tiny dorm bedroom, a woman with hair of the whitest clouds twitched her nose in sleep. A bead of sweat glistened on her pale, freckled forehead before slipping down. She furrowed her brow and turned over.

Dreaming of eerie midnight and nocturnal spirits that ruled the realm of energies, Rize Keer moaned quietly under her duvet. She heard echoes of banging, and rustling, and cursing, believing it was all part of her troubled slumber.

Bang!

Rize flinched in her bed, woken by a cacophony coming from the hallway. Every disturbed lock of her hair shimmered in the moonlight as she trembled. Half-sleeping, she heard another portion of colourful curses that would've made demons applaud.

Heart beating quickly, Rize whispered, "What the…"

Grumbling at whoever had disturbed her at such an early hour, she rubbed her eyes, then blinked to test if her lively imagination created those noises.

Nothing but silence reigned in her flat.

Rize clicked her tongue and covered herself with a duvet, scattering her cloud-white hair over the pillow. A groan slid down her lips while every inch of her body stung with aching soreness after the last painstaking training session. Legs and arms heavy as cast-iron, Rize lay motionless, trying to fall asleep again.

What was I thinking, joining the Academy? she thought. *This training is my death sentence. I hate Rel. I hate all people in this town. Holy elements, my muscles are on fire…*

Rize cursed at everything her eyesight could reach, but a glimpse of a memory brought her back to the place where it had all started.

A vision of Ponktian devoured by flames and thick smokes cooled her anger. The capital of Lalu'Ed civilisation was destroyed when she fled and nothing in her power could reverse that. She lived as a mere human — not talented enough, not influential at all. She was nobody with nothing but uncontrolled magic and resentment.

Head down, Rize thought of the home she had left behind and the ashes that remained. Her eyes stung as she cringed, and a suffocating lump appeared in her throat.

Stop moaning. There's no life for you back there.

The front door of her flat creaked, opening. It knocked against a table with a bulky kettle which, in turn, clattered loudly, reminding her of its presence in the narrow hallway.

"Amethyst, what's going on?" Rize mumbled. "Amethyst?"

She heard a drawn-out sigh and a short grumble in response. The black wildcat seemed asleep, but Rize knew her pet Worock just ignored her.

"Today is our day off…" she muttered and sank in gloom, where her dreams of a quiet weekend faded away. "And I know you're awake. Usually you snort."

Opening one eye, Amethyst granted her a condescending look. "Nonsense."

Rize smirked and climbed out of her warm bed. She shook Amethyst's sleeping place and pulled the cushion out from under him. His retaliation was a swift paw to her backside, leaving a light yet vengeful scratch. Too tired to let out a yelp, she scratched her mildly painful prize with one hand and covered a yawn with the other.

Rize paced swiftly along the cold floor, her bare toes shrinking as they touched it, and opened the door. She paused, standing before an unfamiliar pile of luggage blockading her doorway. A large suitcase, and a range of duffle bags a third of her height, filled the whole space.

"Uh, hello?" she muttered.

Cautious, Rize cast her head around to see where the bags' owner might be, but no one was there to reply. She blinked twice, checking if the bags were just a dream.

"I definitely didn't make those noises up," she said through her grogginess. Tired and irritated, she stared at the offending pile with a glassy look.

Amethyst, as if sensing her confusion, raised his head.

"Go to bed. It's our neighbour...They should've arrived tonight. Rel wrote you two days ago," the cat grumbled sleepily.

"So, you read my mail again and forgot to mention it." She slammed the door and headed back to bed.

"I know you're not angry," Amethyst said, watching Rize crawl back under the duvet.

"I'm furious," she uttered. "I better move my mailbox higher, away from your curious paws," she said and, barely touching the pillow, fell asleep.

But not for long.

A loud and insistent knock came from the door. Rize ignored it and covered her head, though the persistent visitor continued banging.

"Darkness, devour me…" Amethyst sighed, and reluctantly slid down to the floor. He stretched his body and yawned as only felines can. His jaw wide open, the cat released a subtle, hissy exhalation.

"I hear your voice, man! Open up!" insisted a cheerful voice.

Amethyst shambled towards the door and, standing on his hind legs, pulled it open.

"What?" the cat blurted out, annoyed.

The silence lasted so long that Rize couldn't resist her curiosity any longer. Stretching until her joints cracked, she sat up. Blinking, she focused her gaze on the man in the doorway and turned on the light.

He was younger than Rize, or seemed so with soft, perfect tawny skin, accompanied by a delicate mole on his upper lip. In Rize's opinion, that mole could have made anyone seem too flirty. The moment he smiled, his eyes creased, hiding behind the apples of his cheeks. They were young eyes, bright and full of mischief.

"It's not every day you see a Worock opening the door," he said, and his irises sparkled with amber flames of sheer curiosity as he examined the room.

Rize and Amethyst watched the visitor, ready to jump him. Seeing their reaction, the young man gave a baffled giggle and tousled his overgrown black crew cut.

"I think we started from the wrong angle," he said, visibly confused. "Hi, neighbour?"

"Neighbour?" Rize repeated dully. "You're not a girl," she stated.

"And you *are* a girl," he mimicked.

"A promising morning," Amethyst declared in a sombre tone and went back to his sofa. "I'm so proud you've both managed to identify your gender, bipedals."

The newly made roommate stared at the cat with disbelief in his eyes. He stood dumbfounded as if processing that Amethyst dared to comment on his words. Finally, the young man turned his gaze back to Rize.

"Maybe the dorm's administration thought you were a guy," he suggested. "'Cause everyone knows me here."

"And you are?" Rize raised an eyebrow.

"Chour."

"Bless you," Amethyst mocked him.

"I didn't—" the young man said and then slowly sat down on the sofa arm, next to the cat. "Was that a joke?"

Rize sensed trouble. Usually, Worock cats amazed people with their very existence. However, Chour expressed nothing but sheer disbelief that her pet could scoff.

"You should see me dancing," Amethyst retorted. "I'm a bag of talents."

"I bet," Chour played along and gave the cat a weird look. "Anyway. My *name* is Chour. I'm a third-year Academician, a recruit of the Chemistry Department by day and a master of drinks by night."

"Chour…" Rize smiled listlessly and nodded. "I knew I heard it somewhere. Rel told me about you."

"Re-e-e-ally?" His grin could lighten the whole world. "What did he say?"

"Something about your sense of humour," she chuckled. "That I wouldn't get it if my Global language remained at its current level."

"He's right, roomie," Chour agreed, his eyes flickered in a brilliant gleam. "If you're getting to live with me, make sure to go a-a-all the way down every time I want to treat you."

"Why do I need to go down? I'm…I'm not following," Rize frowned.

He laughed, seeing her confusion.

"That was a test," Chour said smugly. "Master of drinks. Tall glasses. Little guilty pleasures…"

Rize observed his hand shaking an imaginary glass with a sour expression on her face. Something in that polishing gesture felt wrong.

"Oh, c'mon!" he said, his arms crossed. "If a man asks you to pull on his horn, you'd ask where he'd left it, wouldn't you?"

"Are we talking about a drinking horn?"

Chour's lips trembled before pursing into a thin, stressed line. Taking a deep breath, he smiled, granting Rize a mocking look.

"Well, that's an awful Global we have here. Let's try the basics. WHA-A-AT IS YO-O-OUR NA-A-AME?" he drawled, raising his voice.

"Please, stop." She rubbed her ear. "I'm Rize, a former mentor. And this brute beast is Amethyst."

"Rize? I've known one Rize," the young man recalled. "But I don't remember anything about her. I have too many customers these days."

"At least you pronounce my name correctly. That's enough for us to get along."

"Everyone call you the food, ha?"

"Exactly," Rize grimaced.

"Did someone dare tease you in the presence of this formidable Worock?" he queried.

"I took part in those teasings, bipedal," Amethyst retorted.

"Bully, then," the neighbour resumed. "I can relate."

"Why did you come?" the cat interrupted his interrogation.

"To make your acquaintance, nothing more."

"Congrats, you've made it. Now get out."

"Bully *and* brute, ha? Hold on! I had a revelation. An excellent name for a cocktail!" Chour nodded approvingly and took out a tiny notepad from his pocket. "I'll make it my signature drink tonight. If only I had enough Brut Champagne..." He started making notes, clearly forgetting that he had invaded somebody's bedroom.

"Why are you still here?" Amethyst asked wearily.

"You know, with such an attitude, you'll have a hard time with the others."

"What others?" Amethyst rolled his eyes.

"With the Worock." He walked away, adding at the door, "They, like you, shun new souls in their society. No — they actually hate them, so…good luck!"

Chour vanished in the darkness of the unlit hallway, but Rize could hear him trying the door to his bedroom.

"Wait," Rize called out. "Are there more Worock cats here? Really?" She held her breath, hoping he wasn't joking.

"Everyone who's anyone is here. It's the Academy, after all. I know about six wildcats." Chour came back, basking in their unbelieving stares. "Odd that you've met none of them."

"We avoid crowded places," Rize explained. "Too many gliders in the town centre."

"Gliders?" Chour half-arched his eyebrow.

"These people who…glide on their…you know, noiseless boards in streets." She pursed her lips. "I should've found out what they were called."

"You're talking about hoverboards. Huh, gliders…" He gasped, theatrically wiping a tear in laughter. "My roomie is Lalu'Edian," he said, and then whispered, "That explains a lot, actually. Anyway, don't worry, your little secret will remain with me."

"W-what are you talking about?" Rize stuttered.

"You don't have a clue, do you? Everyone has been trying to figure out the identity of a recruit, seen along with the Advisor himself. Though Rel hates when I call him by his title, the rest of

Academy Town treats him like a celebrity, so... you know. He always has eyes on him."

"Don't peep a sound," Amethyst thought into her head, creating a telepathic bond.

"Not so chatty anymore, are we?" Chour grinned. "Listen, I'm aware this recruit has a Worock. And I know everyone in this town, except for you. Obviously, Rel made them room us together. Why is he so desperate to hide you away?"

Eyes open, Rize tried to win the staring competition and remained calm. Chour smirked, tilting his head playfully and came closer.

"I've heard the Great One himself was convincing the curious that this recruit wasn't a woman, but a man from Tsaan," he said.

Grim and abrasive, he granted Rize a piercing, surly stare. She had never felt anything like that. Chour's energy — his raw magic, infused by the desire to know — crawled under her skin, trying to find a breach in her mind. As if wandering thorns pierced her muscles, she shrank under his power.

Amethyst hissed, jumping Chour like a predator.

"Keep these tricks to yourself, bipedal!"

"It's not forbidden to read a person, Amethyst," Chour said, wiggling under the huge feline body like a worm.

Carnivorous roar.

"Easy-easy! This will be done to you and Rize many times unless you get yourself some protective trinket at the temple. See? I have one," he waved, showing an old-fashioned ring crowned with green aventurines.

"You're the first man with clairvoyant abilities I've met," she said anxiously, recovering from the attack. "I know it doesn't occur in Tsaan soothsayers only, but still…it's weird."

"This baby-browsing? Nah-Argh!" Chour's bravado changed rapidly after Amethyst's claws pierced his chest. "My gift isn't advanced. I only use it when I work in a pub."

"Master of drinks, of course," Rize guessed, her face grim.

"Can I get up now?" he demanded.

Amethyst squinted but stepped away.

"Thanks. That was…" Chour panted. "Refreshing."

"So," Rize started her own interrogation. "You know everyone's secrets and dark deeds in this town?"

"Only those who like drinking and blathering," he said with an enigmatic smile.

"And you don't tell anyone what you see?" Rize clarified.

"Of course not," Chour got theatrical again. "I honour the master of drinks' code."

"Excellent," Amethyst grumbled. "He has a code."

"You know, guys, I think we'll find common ground despite the rough start. You should come to my pub tonight. I'll introduce you to some nice people, good music, drinks, you name it. Study tour!" Chour said as if nothing had happened. "Any objections?"

"It might be a good idea," Rize thought into Amethyst's head. *"I should meet new people."*

"I hate these bipedal encounters." He sighed, giving up. *"Alright."*

"Where is this pub?" she said, curious.

"I'll leave you my card. The address is there." Chour tapped at the thick piece of paper and stepped back under Amethyst's glare. "C-come at dusk. You won't regret it!"

"I'm sure we will," the cat muttered and ushered his neighbour out of the room.

Chapter 2
CATMEAT RISOTTO

"My lovely Lily," Chour drawled, "please, don't say you're refusing me a discount because I came here with another woman."

Rize shook her head softly, taking a deep breath.

The same morning, her new neighbour insisted on helping her with purchasing a talisman. Protecting herself from the prying eyes of clairvoyants seemed logical after the night incident with Chour. After all, she didn't want it to happen again at the pub.

Spending little time, Rize chose a pendant in the shape of a cat, adorned with rich-violet amethyst. However, the payment part was delayed by her extroverted roommate who miraculously turned shopping into a show.

"Holy elements, you're unbearable." Lily laughed, hand on her chest. "I shouldn't have told you that I'd taken the cloth."

"But you have," he flapped his eyelashes, flipping into drama, "and I'm heartbroken. I still imagine how beautiful our children would've been, you know. This silky hair of yours could make any man—"

Lily cleared her throat and smeared the young man with a patient look, expressing nothing but annoyance.

"We're not on the same team, Chour."

"Not mentioning your generous soul, of course!" He continued as if she said nothing. "You're blessed by the Universe herself with kindness and a soft—"

"Neither compliments nor lies will save you money," Lily cut him off.

He looked sideways and whispered. "What about information?"

What's that supposed to mean? Rize thought.

The merchant pursed her lips as if fighting the temptation to take the bait. Chour winked, playing with the girl, and craned over expensive pieces of jewellery secured in glass caskets.

"Don't you even dare to breathe near those diamonds! It's the latest Runvish collection," Lily hissed, pinching his nose with one hand and putting away jewellery with the other. "And I told you last time that I need nothing from you."

"Not even a fresh rumour about your boss?" he smirked.

Honouring the master of drinks' code? Yeah, right. Rize crossed her arms. *Windbag.*

"I'll be dead if the High Priestess finds out I'm doing favours for a drunkard again," Lily said, her voice going down to a whisper.

"That's amazing, because you'll be giving a discount to this poor Lalu'Edian girl," Chour said, smiling as if his life depended on this bargain. "She's so broke that she wears an academy uniform on weekends. See? She has no threads!"

Rize shifted her weight from one foot to the other, feeling uncomfortable under the merchant's stare. She was reading her. Rize had few clothes but never thought it was a problem.

I should've come here alone, she thought, shivering from the icy wash of Lily's clairvoyant energy surges under her skin. *Interesting...Chour's energy felt different.*

"Lalu'Edian, huh?" Lily tilted her head. "Your kind never linger here."

Rize shrugged.

"It's all for the greater good." Chour took Lily's hand. Rize could swear his eyes got misty. "The High Priestess will understand you did it out of love."

Lily glared at the man as if burning him to divine ashes was one of her newfound religious duties.

"I'll pay in full," Rize insisted, tired of the awkward scene.

"Are you sure?" he raised his voice.

His eyes widened, signalling to stay quiet. It had been a long time since Rize had listened to a man's orders willingly, and she certainly wasn't about to start again now.

"That's alright. I'm sur—"

"And she's humble too!" he exclaimed. Glass caskets and the treasures inside them trembled in disturbed unison. "Isn't it worth your mercy, Lily?"

"Darkness, devour me…" Rize pinched her nose, ashamed. "Chour, let me pay for this stupid talisman and I'll go."

"Over my dead body!" He hopped to a shopfront and stretched his legs, trying to win Lily's attention back. "Which is divine, don't you think?"

The merchant pushed him down and giggled, suppressing contagious laughter.

"What guy can drive people mad and make them laugh at the same time?" she wondered.

"A nice one?" Chour croaked, lying on the floor.

"I can't sell enchanted pieces for a smaller price, dear," Lily looked at Rize with a guilty smile. "I'll lose my job if I do."

"Sorry, roomie. My haggling has never failed me before," Chour said, standing up like his back was broken in three places at once.

"Must be your bad day," Lily deadpanned, still looking at Rize. "Tell me your name. I'll connect your bank account to my system."

Confused, Rize glanced at Chour and back at the merchant. "I'm sorry…I don't…"

"You're still willing to pay, right?" Lily said, gently tapping in the price on her glass screen. "Or you can give me your *shard*."

"You're forgetting, she's Lalu'Edian, my love." Chour chuckled. "Okay, roomie. Academy Town has its own banking system. It's connected to all public places, so if you forgot your shard…" he paused, enjoying himself too much. "Lily can find your name in her little glass screen and request money from the bank."

"Directly?" Rize furrowed.

"Yes, dear," the merchant smiled. "Though, I'll need your fingerprint to approve the transaction."

"I know how to use this." Rize took out a small glass card from her chest pocket. "Will it work here?"

"Oh, so you have your shard. Excellent!" Lily tapped the card to her screen and it beeped quietly. "Done. Now let me wrap up the talisman and you're ready to go."

"No-no. Wait." Chour snatched it from her hands. "She'll put it on here. Allow me."

The young man came up and gently threw the silver chain over her neck. His breath too close to her ear, Rize tensed but said nothing.

"Don't worry, my lady. I won't touch you."

Rize heard his soft chuckle from behind her back and took a deep breath.

"No one has called me that since I left my parent's house," she said, finding his courtesy amusing.

"A-ha…" Victorious, he clasped the necklace and let the pendant slide down the chain with a chirpy jangle. "So, you grew up in a noble family."

Ugh…Don't tell more than people ask of you. Rel's voice echoed in Rize's head. Her lips pursed, she nodded. Learning a lesson the hard way wasn't her favourite thing. *My neighbour is gathering intel on me. Great.*

"You know, I felt there was something in you," Chour said matter-of-factly, stepping aside to have a good look at her. "Yes. It's the prideful posture. What do you think, Lily?"

"I think her past is none of your business," the merchant said. "How do you feel, dear? Sometimes talismans need to adjust to a new owner."

"The metal is warm," Rize noticed and touched her pendant.

"Good! You're connecting with it already. Also, you might get a slight headache or a temperature until it becomes fully active."

"I'll keep it in mind. Thank you." Rize looked at her talisman and giggled. "I'm sure Amethyst will mock me for it."

"Who's Amethyst?" Lily asked curiously.

"My overreacting cat."

Lily's eyebrows went up, disappearing behind her blunt fringe. "A cat that can mock, so…a talking cat? You have a Worock?"

Shut up, Rize. Shut up. Just shut up. She nodded quietly, clenching her jaws harder than before.

"Shopping is over!" Chour pushed her to the exit. "Funny that you knew nothing about the Academy financial system, roomie."

"Shopping wasn't a part of Rel's curriculum." Rize rolled her eyes.

Lily gaped at her and then at Chour in disbelief. "She's one of Rel's people?!"

Chour narrowed his eyes, his chest twitched in silent laughter.

"Don't remember saying such a thing." He smiled enigmatically and opened a door, letting Rize out. "Bye, Lily!"

"Why haven't you told me? Hey!" the merchant yelled at their backs. "Chour! Argh, you, nasty demon!"

The door shut loudly and Chour dragged Rize away, while she protested against his further supervision. The moment they turned down a less crowded alley, he burst into hysterical laughter.

"You're a shining gem for a spy, you know that?" he said after having a good laugh.

"None of that would've happened if I came there alone!" she retorted, adding, "Rel will kill me."

"Nah. Lily won't pass this to anyone," Chour assured her. "She likes gossip but spreading it will cast her out from her priesthood."

"Why?"

"Priestesses are supposed to keep confessions in secret from the mortal realm," he explained. "They are the ears of our loving Universe, not her mouth."

"Convenient." Rize hid her face in her hands and sighed. "You did it on purpose. You led me to her to see what exactly?"

"How you communicate when you think you're safe," he said. "I like examining people, you know. Even some innocent shopping can tell a lot about you."

"Charming," she hissed as they reached the front gates of their dorm. "I don't like you, Chour," she stated.

"Why? 'Cause I honestly tell you about my intentions?" he looked at her with pity. "You'll understand soon enough that I'm the most honest and open person in this town. You'll love me."

"You trade private information!"

"Oh, well, that's just vulgar." Chour seemed offended but then smiled mockingly. "I exchange it for something of value. Could be meaningless rumours, could be life-saving hints. You never know what you might find on the bottom of a glass."

"Remind me to never drink with you," Rize grumbled.

"Doubt it's possible to avoid my humble company in this place. Speaking of which," he shuffled his last step, "I need to go to work."

They stopped at a small courtyard, surrounded by cherry trees. Rize's glance became softer watching floating petals. The warm season threatened to end soon. She could see it in the flowers stripping their fragile clothes and throwing them down to the cold ground, paved with stone tiles and dust. A gust of wind troubled the trees, lingered in their crowns, and descended to play with her hair. She stood motionless, wind messing with her wavy strands.

Chour's lips quivered in a smile.

"Who's frightened you so much that your hair became white, girl?"

"Oh, get lost in a hollow…"

She marched away, puffing with anger.

"See you tonight at my pub, then!" he said, clearly happy with himself.

"Yeah, right," she grumbled.

Storming through corridors and stairs, Rize swiftly got to her flat and slammed the door so hard that a clunky kettle in her hallway fell from its place to the floor.

"I see you enjoyed your time," Amethyst said, coming to his mistress.

Rize left his comment unnoticed. She took off her shoes, leaned on the door, and slowly slid down, trying to cool her head.

"I always said that shopping is too draining to consider it good leisure. Did you buy a talisman?"

"Look," she panted, showing off the new trinket on her chest. "Now you'll guard me everywhere I go."

Amethyst eyed the violet stone that swung from a fine chain before him.

"I like it."

"Well, isn't that a relief?" Rize muttered, stretching her legs. "Thankfully, I don't have to go anywhere else today."

"Long nap in bed?"

"Super long nap in bed, my furry friend," she said and shuffled towards her room.

The day was filled with the quiet motions of her pet and the musty scent of old books until the luminaries had sufficiently fallen, and it was finally time to meet Chour and his friends. Forced out of bed to put on her only dress, Rize headed to the pub accompanied by two amethysts.

"I'm not an expert, but in my opinion, you need new clothes," Amethyst presumed, examining her dress that had not been worn since the Blossom Feast. "You may have cleaned it up of soot and ashes, but the hem is still ruined. I don't recall human females wearing torn attire. You could wear your uniform. At least it's neat."

"Yeah, and you should smile more," Rize brushed him off. "That's the place. Looks ancient."

They lingered before the entrance for a brief inspection. The cross-hipped roof of the pub was shingled with a greyish slate that gleamed with lamppost light after rain. The building looked old but charming in its own mysterious way. Covered by a vast, green ivy carpet, its white walls and dark wood beams welcomed and lured everyone who glimpsed it.

"Let's go." She watched one of the *gliders* parking his hoverboard near the entrance and quailed at its magnetic glow. "Inside. Now."

Rize opened the door, and a long-forgotten harmony of sounds overwhelmed her. She forgot how loud a pub can be. Live music, loud chatting, roaring laughter, clinking glasses, the whispering foam of fizzy drinks, and creaking chairs. She paced through the hall, her shoes sticking to the dirty floor with every step.

"Ugh, gross," she winced.

"I'll make you wash my paws after this," Amethyst thought. *"Chour's working at the bar. What's our plan?"*

"Avoid drinking, but meet people?"

"And cats," he added, coming closer to their neighbour. *"Here goes nothing."*

"Finally, you're here!" Chour beamed as Rize hopped on a stool. "Guys, meet Rize!"

Three academicians waved to her.

"So, it's Rice?" a bearded man said and a silly grin stuck to his face. "Like food?"

"What's your name again?" Amethyst asked.

"Khan."

"Shut up, Khan."

The two girls who sat next to him sprayed drinks out of their mouths and choked with laughter. Rize stroked her pet, hiding a smile.

"I told you, he's different." Chour chuckled, grabbing a cloth to wipe excess liquid from the counter. "Amethyst, come here. I've prepared a place for you."

The cat took a seat on a soft padded chair designed specifically for Worock cats. It was so tall that Amethyst could easily put his front limb on the counter.

"If I were drunk, I could confuse you with one of my regular customers," Chour said, amused. "He's also black and hairy...likes to place his elbows on smooth surfaces."

"I wonder how far you'd go with this joke if I let you, bipedal." Amethyst killed his smile with one predatory gaze.

"An-anyway," the young man stuttered, "local Worocks would've ignored us. They never interact with strangers. Not to mention that talking is something that requires their respect."

"That's xenophobic," Amethyst said. "I see nothing bad in disrespecting you out loud."

"Me, and many others, I guess," Chour noted and passed Rize a tall glass with a shimmering blue drink. "Enjoy your cocktail. I'll be right back."

Croaking under pressure, he lifted a box filled with dirty glasses from the floor and left for the kitchen.

"He's so hardworking," a woman said dreamily and craned closer to Rize. "Usually we do handshakes, but Chour warned us you're a Lalu'Edian."

She had styled her black hair in a blunt cut bob. It looked bizarre and made Rize stare at her a bit longer than she should have.

"How very thoughtful of him," Rize grumbled, quitting her rude gaping.

"I'm Neeka," the woman smiled. "That's my stupid brother, Khan. And that's his girlfriend, Moira."

"Hey…" she raised her glass.

"What now?" Amethyst thought into Rize's head. *"They tell us their whole bloodline?"*

Rize cleared her throat, hiding a chuckle. "Nice to meet you."

Chour came back, his eyes glistening mischievously.

"Something nice for your pet," he whispered showing a bundle of strange green grass in his hand.

"It's Amethyst, right?" Neeka leaned on the counter to see the cat better.

"Yes."

"Have you met other Worocks?"

"No."

"Do you like it here?"

"Barely."

Neeka paused, confused, and looked at Moira — she shrugged.

"You don't need to answer if you're not feeling like talking."

"I am, though you pick weird topics."

"Sorry?" she frowned.

"Just calm down, alright?" Rize said to her pet. "Here. Chour made you something."

"A triple dosage of catnip I hope," Khan muttered to his glass.

Amethyst smelled the greenish liquid in the bowl placed before him. "Is that...*milk*?"

"Just give it a try. Please?" Chour drawled. "I'm shocked you're so stubborn."

"Poor you," the cat deadpanned. He lapped his drink a bit and raised his head, ears flattened. "Tastes like bitter dandelions."

"Is it good or bad?" Rize raised her eyebrow.

"It's grass, dearie," Amethyst closed the subject, looking around. "It would be nice to meet someone of *my* kind now. Where are the others, Chour? You promised me six cats."

The young man looked sideways to check the place and sighed. "Sorry to disappoint you, Meatball, but there're none here tonight."

"Meatball?" Amethyst said, his ears erected. "You must have a death wish, bipedal."

"Hey, it's just a cute nickname. I give them to all my customers!" Chour poured himself a drink and had a sip, pondering. "Considering your mistress's name, though…"

"It's actually hilarious." Khan snorted. "Rice with a meatball."

"To catmeat risotto!" Chour raised a toast, splashing his drink on Rize.

Chapter 3
I LEAKED

"Not saying I'm crushed by it but," Amethyst looked up at his mistress, "you're quiet this morning. What's up?"

"I swear," Rize howled on the way to the stadium, "if someone asks me again 'Rice? Like food?', I'll curse that person."

"It's not worth it, Rize," Amethyst assured her, coming closer in the fading dark. "Pay no attention. Or laugh with them! Self-deprecation is a crucial trait for a woman."

"A misogynistic scoffing from a cat? Yeah, sounds like a perfect start to the day." Rize paused, checking the awakening horizon. "If people behaved like that to you, I doubt you would giggle."

"I'm a darling, who would make fun of me?" Amethyst said. "Come on. Rel's already at the stadium. I can smell His Hooded Excellency from a mile away."

"I don't think we should mention that here," Rize whispered. "Even in jest."

The cat agreed, his ears flattened. "The wilderness has benefited you, after all. Your caution speaks for itself."

A few days had passed since the test in the Nightmare Lands, which Rize had failed in the worst way possible. She'd set out to find her custodian and ended up forging a pact with an ancient demon. At first, the agreement seemed harmless. What evil could possibly come from one's shared stories? But Rel had another opinion about it. He forbade her even think about meeting the demon again.

"Stop poking me." Rize grimaced. "Both of us must learn to keep our mouths shut. Rel has a point, even though his flair for the dramatic is annoying."

"Boo-hoo," Amethyst drawled. "Guess you're happy to have a telepathic cat now."

She rolled her eyes. "I'm on the cloud."

Rize kindled the thought of seeing the demon called Koryn, and not because of the pact. Their meeting changed her, twisting and shuffling the moral fibre of her very soul.

The memory of that fateful night and its life-shifting choices filled Rize's mind once again. How thrilling that had been. She realized, with a little shame and a trill of excitement, that she would give anything to experience that adrenaline surge again. Being a creator of all roads in her life was the sweetest sip of freedom she had never had before.

"Ugh." One hand on her belly, Rize staggered as if someone punched her guts.

"M?" the cat looked up at her.

"What the demon?" She stared at her wrist, enveloped by blurry threads of buzzing energy. "Amethyst!" she yelped as the unknown magic started to spread.

An otherworldly matter grasped her arms, drawing her towards something beyond. She smelled salt in the air, heard seagulls cry above the ocean. Or did she see them?

Desperate to stand still, Rize staggered again. Her face grimaced in agony as she let out a groan. Head craned, she finally fell to her knees, gasping for air. Something burned her insides. The air scratched her lungs like a thousand thorns multiplying in her chest.

Her spine arched with a chilling crack, and a cry full of pain left her chest. No one seemed to hear it.

"Try to calm down!" Amethyst paced in circles, unable to help. "Help! Anybody!"

They were alone. The dorm was far behind and the stadium seemed too far.

Rize coughed blood, staining the ground in crimson.

"I got this," she panted, her lips tasted iron. "Stay with me."

"I'm here." He entered her mind. *"Always."*

Eyes closed, Rize fought the invasion the only way that was left.

"That's *my* body," she said through gritted teeth.

Supplied with strong emotions, Rize channelled her inner flow. Storming energy destabilised her magic and that meant one thing — she must act fast to prevent her demonic canker from spreading.

I'm not becoming a demon today. She shook off the sensation, taking back control of her mind and body. *Get. Out!*

It ended as fast as it had started. Throbbing muscles and a thin layer of blood on her lips reminded her the seizure was real.

"Holy elements…" Rize face-planted on the dusty ground. "I thought I'd die."

She breathed in cool air hungrily. It tickled her lungs, floating up and down her throat.

"What in the Universe was that?" Amethyst wondered, shaking. "Was that…a portal? In your body?!"

"Felt like a good old possession if you ask me." Rize slowly got on her feet. "I've seen it happen once to one of my brothers. Nasty thing to clean up, you know. He's never been the same after it."

"You disappeared!" the cat freaked out, ignoring her nostalgia. "And then came back!"

"That would explain the seagulls." She frowned, trying to focus. "The Dolmen magic no doubt. It pulled me in, but I slipped out. I'm in full control."

"Sorry that I'm not pouncing out of happiness!" Amethyst snorted at his paws. "I knew that *thing* would do something like that."

"That thing's name is Koryn," she said. "And it was my doing that started the process. I mean...I guess it was my thoughts about meeting him."

"Oh, so now you miss the charming landscapes of the Nightmare Lands?" the cat retorted. "Remember I said you became more cautious? I take it back."

"Amethyst, he's not bad!" Rize threw her hands and a splash of water hit the ground. She stared at her glistening palm in surprise.

"Don't you see?" he yelped. "Somehow, he hooked your demonic canker! One wrong turn. One flawed emotion and your own magic would absorb your soul. That's it!"

"I won't become a demon," Rize said. "I took control back. It's fine."

Amethyst narrowed his eyes, treating her with silent disapproval.

"What?" she raised her voice. "I'm fine! See?"

"Just..." Amethyst swallowed curses and headed to the stadium. "Unbelievable."

"I'm sure it's nothing," she mumbled. "Must be a new symptom of my self-control issues." She shook off dripping water and wiped her hand on her combat trousers, graciously provided by Rel with the rest of the Academy uniform.

"Say that to Rel." The cat looked back, his eyes flashing furiously. "Don't forget to explain why your mouth is full of blood."

Fingers trembling, she swiftly wiped her lips.

"That's unfair, Amethyst."

"Don't teach me about the unfairness of this world," he said. "I was forced to be around your kind. And you...you just moan about the injustice like a spoiled child."

"I doubt your mother would want you to die in that forest," she retorted. "It was me who worked to feed you. I was twelve! Or did you forget that my parents wanted to throw you out? You live because of *my* foolish stubbornness."

"Careful, dearie. Your pride is showing."

Rize groaned in annoyance but followed her pet to the stadium without further blathering.

"You said you were thinking about that demon," Amethyst recalled. "What was on your mind?"

"Our agreement," she said, plunging into her memories again. "How we've met." Her heart skipped a beat. "That day in general."

"Your hand is watering the road." Amethyst pricked his ears, hearing a strange sound. "I wonder what's happened with the lightning and fire."

They entered the stadium grounds. The dawn followed the pair, lighting the field where Rel was waiting, still and straight as a lifeless statue. He stood with all the flawless control over body and mind that only a custodian could display. Rel was a perfect example of a fighter, a custodian to the Citadel squad, the Great One's mystic advisor and…a second Great One — an anomaly that had occurred only once before in the World's history. An anomaly that once led to a World War.

To hide the fact of his existence, problematic as it was, Rel never took off his hood, obscuring the wide gash of a sign that adorned his forehead. It (along with the overgrown fringe) prevented the global war that would ensue should his secret ever be discovered. The sign of greatness could be borne by only one, who supervised developed lands so the peace might reign.

If the peoples had found out that Rel was a bearer, it would mean the Universe, their one true goddess, failed to guide them. Living in a world forgotten by the divine could bring only changes.

The Citadel and its Elders hated changes. The only person who despised them more was Rel himself. Neither the Great One nor Rel could fathom why the Elders were so jumpy about him. Eal loved the attention and ruling seemed natural to him, while Rel's biggest ambition was to have a lovely holiday away from the Citadel grounds. Completely alone.

Granting passers-by a polite grin, Rel watched the other early birds at the stadium. He smoothed his fringe under the hood and, hearing footsteps, turned around.

"Hey, Catmeat Risotto!" he waved them. "Move. Today's going to be a long and hard day for you."

"Risotto?" Rize raised her eyebrow. "Seriously?"

"Would you prefer '*Rice* and a meatball'?" Rel smiled mockingly.

"I'll kill Chour," the cat said, looking sideways as if their neighbour could suddenly appear next to him. "Does he report to you our every step too?"

"Relax, Amethyst," Rel chuckled. "I popped into the pub last night. Chour's friends were literally squealing with delight that they'd met a new Lalu'Edian and a Worock who can crack jokes."

"Since we're on the subject," Rize mumbled. "Why do I live with Chour?"

"He's a responsible lad—"

"He's nothing but a rat! And trades private information too!" she fumed.

"He does…what?" Amethyst looked at her. "Why didn't you tell me?"

"Both of you are full of resentment…as usual," Rel said. "Chour is a spy. *My* spy, so to speak, and he's a responsible one. I don't need others paying too much attention to you two." He sighed. "Especially after what happened in the wilderness."

Her brows furrowed, Rize nodded and quietly headed to a track.

"Yeah, about that," Amethyst uttered, making his human halt. "Rize has a new thing with her hand."

"What?" Rel lowered his voice, though he looked like he wanted to smash Rize in one punch. "Are you telling me you ruined everything we've worked on?"

Rize gulped.

"I leaked just before the training. I mean, not me. Of course, not me," she mumbled, expecting a thunderous response. "My hand."

"You…leaked?" He coughed, though Rize could swear she heard a chuckle. "Have you noticed anything else? Funny heartbeats, occasional breathlessness, a tickling in your belly?" Rel interrogated her smugly.

"How did you—" Rize whispered.

"I bet your blood is," the custodian held the intrigue and smiled, "running faster right now. You almost feel it burns your skin. Are you having daydreams?"

She nodded.

"Well, at least it's a well-known problem," Amethyst stopped Rel's scoffing. "What's causing that?"

"Oh," Rel drawled with admiration. "Your human has a pash on someone. And now, five laps, easy jog! Chop-chop!" He clapped. "I should think now. Promise me you won't hurt Chour. I care about him."

"Don't be silly, Rel. I met him once!" Rize said.

"Right," he nodded. "Is it me who must worry about your heart then?" he grinned again.

"You should anyway. Her heart's so small, it barely pumps her blood. Why do you think she's so pale all the time?" Amethyst said.

Rel laughed. "Small or not, Meatball. She's in love."

"I can't be. I know nothing about it. And I've never wanted to discover that, to be honest," Rize protested.

"Aw, you're blushing," Rel said. "It's adorable. You're adorable."

"Stop it," she hissed, calling to his reason. "I have a problem. You're supposed to help me restore my inner flow, not to add more wounds with stupid jokes."

Rel crossed his arms and went silent for a moment.

"You're starting to sound like my squad healer," Rel said. "I believe it's a good sign, Risotto. Your spirit has almost patched itself up."

"Does it mean I'm not dangerous anymore and you're letting us go?" she said dreamily.

"Don't be ridiculous," he winced. "I want you to meet my fighters and, considering that nothing awaits you in Ponktian, staying here is your best option to live your life, not survive in the suburbs."

"Sounds reasonable..." Amethyst muttered, taking Rel's side.

"My healer will examine your leaking problem. We'll fix it and then you can do whatever you want," Rel said and yawned as if she bored him. "Holy elements, I'm tired! I'll take a day off tomorrow. Whatever happens while I'm away, make sure this 'not-love', undiscovered emotion remains under control, alright? Try not to flip out or something."

Chapter 4
OBSESSIONS
Chour

"Grant was disappointed you didn't come to the stadium, Rize," Amethyst said.

Chour heard him barely moving his legs after the morning training.

No mercy, ha. That's the Grant I know, he thought and turned over in his bed.

Fake snore.

"Ugh, he is disgusting," the cat said.

"Most men snore, Amethyst," Rize muttered.

"Don't remind me of your brothers…"

Snoring peacefully, Chour ensured that no one would catch him eavesdropping. He was barely awake after the night shift, though his old habits kept him up. Frankly, they were the only reason he walked the World in the first place. His secrets protected him better than anything.

"Anyway," Amethyst continued, "if Rel is absent, you should practise alone. Grant's words, not mine."

Instinctively, Chour tensed his ears. He had left his door open to catch whatever secrets his roommates might discuss, and finally he heard something worth his time.

Has Rel told them about his departure? He informed them and not me? Chour frowned. Something nasty swirled inside his chest, wrapping his heart in acidic ropes of jealousy.

He huffed.

"Did you know," Rize ignored her pet's words, "the Monok civilisation had been using intangible repositories instead of ordinary libraries to store all knowledge about the World?"

"And where do you think they keep it?" Amethyst said sceptically. "In a cloud? Don't make me laugh. These placators just fool half of the World's population by telling tales."

His lips pursed. Chour stopped breathing for his own sake. He planted his face into the pillow and shook with silent, convulsive laughter.

Poor Lalu'Edians… Amethyst can't imagine how right he is.

Eventually, Chour's throat betrayed him. A short chuckle echoed across his empty bedroom, making Rize and Amethyst lower their voices.

"Can I read in silence?" she muttered. "Chour gave me this screen till tomorrow. I want—"

The cat's nails scratched the floor.

A subtle groan of pain came out of Rize's chest, and the fight began.

"Get off of my sofa," Amethyst grunted.

"You're heavy," she moaned as if crushed. "No-no-no! Careful with the screen!"

The cat hissed and the muffled sound of textile pillows scattering across the floor announced his victory.

"It's my sofa, bipedal!"

"Argh…Let me stretch my legs for Universe's sake!"

The sound of chirpy cracks forced Chour to cringe.

Someone needs to see a healer with these joints, he thought. *Wait. I'm a healer! Should make a balm for her knees. Ha-ha.* A snide smile stuck to his face. *One more thing to trade — one more secret to gather.*

While Chour praised his genius manipulation skills, Amethyst began purring, filling the place with a loud, warm rumble.

"So, our neighbour graciously gave you an opportunity to catch up with modern technologies," the cat said, his voice full of bile.

"You hate him, huh?" Rize said. "I'm shocked. Now, let me read in peace."

"You can hide behind this glassy board as much as you like. I won't change the subject," Amethyst retorted. "You must continue your training, especially after what happened yesterday. Has your hand acted normally since then?"

Hand? Hm…

Like a worm, Chour wiggled closer to the door with the most peaceful snoring he could mimic. His obsession to know everything about anything could compete with Rel's control issues.

"Amethyst, stop poking me." Rize hissed in pain. "Great. I have a scratch now."

"Answer the question."

Clearly annoyed, she put the glass screen aside with a loud thud.

"Why are we here?" Rize asked.

"O-o-oh…" the cat drawled. "I see. A philosopher bit you while I was away. You shouldn't have opened the door to a stranger."

"I'm serious." Rize said. "Why are we here?"

Good question…

Chour stared at the ceiling, waiting for Amethyst's reply. The old paint had long spun a cobweb of cracks and spoiled the view. Dwelling over his head, those shattered branches reflected his guesses better than anything.

Rize was damaged. He'd be a poor bartender if he hadn't got a sense for the souls with spirit voids. These people could spend a fortune within one night. Hurt and lonely — they were good for his business. Still, he failed to understand Rel's plan.

What was Rize to him? An expendable tool? An act of charity or a remission of guilt? The questions buzzed in his head, making it impossible to think clearly.

"What's on your mind?" Amethyst said after an awkward silence.

Rize sighed. Shortly, her breathing quavered.

"I-it's b-been," she stuttered nasally. "It's been amusing and unusual, but meeting with Koryn—"

"With a demon," Amethyst corrected her.

A DEMON?! Chour flinched in his bed.

"With the guardian," Rize suggested a neutral word. "It got me thinking about our safety. I don't want to be here."

"Care to clarify?" the cat said. "You don't mean the dorm, do you?"

"I don't want to get up before dawn and leave all my strength at the stadium or arena. I don't want to come back to this stone box being wet and smelly, while there," — she waved her hand to the side — "in Ponktian, a whole house awaits me with comfortable furniture and no loud roommates."

Chour took it as an invitation and reproduced the best snoring in timbre and volume that could only be made after a brief moment of hesitation.

"Can't say I disagree," Amethyst grumbled. "Still…you didn't answer my question, dearie. How's your hand?"

"It's fine," she muttered. "We should go home. We don't belong here."

His feet light and quiet, Chour reached the hallway and leaned against the wall. Fully absorbed in the drama, he bit his knuckles in anticipation. However, her next words calmed him.

"I'm against staying in a town, where a faulty Great One bullies me so that I can run faster, swing weapons harder, or concentrate better. I refuse to pledge my loyalty to the Citadel. Now that no one tries to corner me, I have nothing to fight for." Rize took a pause to blow her nose. "I don't care what the Council would do to me. I want to go home, where sisters despise my apathy, and brothers call out for drinks every Friday night and I refuse to go because I *can*."

She sobbed, her voice cracked with every exhale.

"Nope," Amethyst protested. "Not the wet eyes. You know I hate it."

"Sorry," Rize whispered and took a deep breath.

Chour froze, listening to her unsteady breathing. His eyes threatened to pop out. He mulled over the next steps carefully, though every fibre of his being wanted to spit acidic curses.

The rumours about Lalu'Ed were true, then. She must be one of the few who survived the attack. But why is she here? He shook his head. Overwhelmed by the fact that Rel shared his secret so recklessly and then hid all of it from his squad. *None of the Geckos knew about Rize and Amethyst. Does it mean Rel saved her single-handedly? A madman.*

A moment passed. Then it clicked.

His temperature dropped as sheer fear clenched his heart, squishing it like a stress toy. Chour looked back to the cupboards where he stashed all his ingredients and herbs. He squinted as if it could help him unsee the truth. He was tricked, too eager to earn more when Rel brought a small fortune to his pub.

Drinking daily, avoiding people, having no interest in his squad, obsession over new contacts, talking to himself, being chirpy like a girl with a new doll... He recalled Rel's recent behaviour which he had failed to connect together.

Indeed, it made little sense that the advisor sent the best people away 'to rest' for the whole summer.

Idiots!

He pinched his nose, trying to find his strengths and wits. After all, he needed those to protect the silly girl and her jumpy cat from now on.

Rel stopped taking his herbs again. He sighed. *Risotto...Poor thing.*

Chapter 5
'FILTHY BROOM' RULE

Amethyst crawled up Rize's body, facing her eyes. Wet and glossy, they mirrored the fears of an irresponsible child who sabotaged her self-confidence.

It sickened Rize that she had to deal with the consequences of her choices. The very thought frightened her deeply. She had burnt the bridges a long time ago but refused to admit that she had no other place to stay and no one to trust except her cat.

"We're stuck here together. Stop acting like you're alone in this mess," Amethyst said, resting his head on her shoulder. "If you want, I'll ask Grant to arrange our way back home. He could pull this off. He's a custodian, after all." He looked into her sad eyes and asked softly, "How do you like this idea?"

"Disgusting." Chour threw himself into the hallway.

Accidentally clashing the furniture on his way to Rize's bedroom, he interrupted Rize speaking her mind. His face was crumpled, eyes red, and the overall look seemed a bit malicious. It took him ages to put everything back into its place. Finally, the sleepy young man shuffled straight to Rize's bed and fell face down into the pillow.

Confused, Rize and Amethyst watched him from the sofa as if Chour was a dangerous beast on the loose.

"Are you sure you're in the right room?" Amethyst pricked his ears. "Sincerely hope you didn't fall asleep, bipedal."

Rolling over onto his back, Chour rubbed his eyes and groaned as if someone had put a crate with stones onto his chest.

"I woke up just in time to hear the end of your conversation," he said. "No, I wasn't standing at the door *on purpose*. I went out to drink some water. I'm absolutely parched in the morning, guys...And my coordination...Well, get used to it."

"What do you want, Chour?" Rize asked, holding her tears. A short, uncontrolled gasp escaped her chest as she uttered his name.

"Do I hear a stuffy nose?" He sat, blinking. "Are you crying? Oh, your face is like a swollen beetroot, girl!"

"Get. Out." Amethyst hissed. "It's hay fever."

"No offence, Meatball," — Chour smirked, stretching — "flowering ended one month ago in this region. And I bribed a healer to get her medical record. She's not allergic to anything." He rubbed his neck and got out of bed, ignoring their baffled looks. "I suppose you won't cope without the irreplaceable me. Let's go. I'm an expert in eliminating bad moods." He shook the sofa where they rested. "Come on! Get up! My great-grandmother, peace to her soul, was faster than you two."

Amethyst gently slid down to the floor, allowing his human to follow their neighbour. Rize stepped, her feet heavy and tired. She lingered before the threshold of his bedroom, glancing over the place with a critical look on her face.

"Wow," she said, her voice still nasally. "I thought your room would look different."

"Did you expect piles of rubbish, dirty socks, and empty kegs of beer all over the floor? I could arrange that if it cheers you up," Chour said. He approached a small hanging cabinet.

"Something like that," she muttered.

Rize squeezed through the doorway and carelessly sat down on a high bed which barricaded the entrance. She gave the room a judgemental look, trying to understand what kind of man was her roommate.

Chour's dwelling seemed too humble even for her tastes. There was absolutely nothing apart from a bed, a table with a barstool and three hanging cabinets. The absence of the furniture made it spacious and cold while colourful pictures of various fruits, herbs, and exotic vegetables covered every wall.

Numerous collages, prints, and handwritten texts hung loose, rustling softly when someone passed by them. Chour seemed boring, even invisible, standing right next to them. Clearly, that was the pictures' purpose — to distract and cloud the mind.

Rize wasn't an exception. Curious, her eyes wandered from one wall to another. She discerned pages with unfamiliar formulas, and notes which referred to essences' side effects on humans. The only relatively normal and understandable pictures were brightly decorated posters that exposed obscure mottos.

'Don't be a goose. Pour some juice!'. *'Forget saying 'cheers' unless air meets the bottom'*, Rize read odd lines, raising an eyebrow. *'I'm a distillation fan'? And I thought I'm strange.*

"Well?" Chour grabbed a dense, white cloth and wiped a tall glass till it shined in the sunlight. "Judging by what I've heard, you want to cut and run."

Rize remained silent, as did Amethyst, resting at her feet.

"Being homesick is natural here," Chour reassured them, taking another glass from the cabinet. "Not to mention the tiredness. When I got here for the entrance exams, the first thought that came into my mind was, 'What am I doing here? Why did I get myself into this?'"

Taking a dramatic pause, he opened the corner cabinet. Holding his breath, he carefully took out an antique marble mortar with its pestle from the shelf and put them aside. Thinking no more, he grabbed fresh bunches of mint and basil. He threw the herbs over his shoulder as if knowing that they would land onto the table.

Once everything was ready, he came up to the wall with the formulas. His gaze slid over the recipes, looking for something, jumping from one note to another.

Watching someone who had everything in its place and in order would usually bore Rize to death. Oddly, his prepping routine calmed her instead.

"There you are!" Chour spotted an old, yellowed page and carefully tore the faded formula from the wall. "You can't hide from me."

"How did you cope with…you know," — Rize gestured around — "all of that?"

"I have a guess," Amethyst said. "He started working in a pub and became a drunkard."

"Assure you, my furry friend, I prefer other ways of running away from problems." Chour chuckled. "I attended classes and trainings, but it brought me nothing but disappointment. I barely passed the annual exams," he said. "Answering your question, Rize, I didn't cope at all. Our common friend rescued me."

"Rel?" she assumed.

Chour nodded. His moves gentle, he took out berries, fruits, and other components for a drink. Finally, he dropped a pill into a jug of still water, making the liquid fizz.

Show-off, Amethyst thought into her head.

Rize's lips quivered in a smile as a white wisp appeared on the water's bubbly surface. It swirled in a wild, captivating dance. Soon enough, it slid down the jug like a fluffy ball of mist, then crashed at the tabletop, leaving nothing but a wet spot behind.

"Once I passed the final exam by the skin of my teeth," Chour continued, throwing a slice of freshly chopped green apple into his mouth, "my mates dragged me to a cooking workshop. I'll explain.

After the seminar, a grand tasting was promised, and I never shun handouts. A free meal is a free meal."

"Yeah-yeah, we know something about poverty and famine," Amethyst rolled his eyes. "Cut to the chase, dramatist."

"Really?" Chour distracted. "I've heard Lalu'Edian households thrive and feast no matter the season."

"As I said, I stopped being a lady of the house when I left my family." Rize shrugged. "Considering that Amethyst is always hungry, and he's a picky eater—"

"Nonsense!" the cat protested. "Though, please, don't add that rubbish you spiced my milk with last time."

"How dare you?" Chour wrinkled his nose. "It was valerian! Cats like it!"

"Well, I'm special."

"What about some catnip?" Chour said. "Everyone loves catnip."

"Doubt I will."

Chour winked, pulling herbs from the depth of the shelf. "We'll see."

"So, what happened at the seminar?" Rize asked, curious.

"Right," Chour nodded, crushing some mint in a mortar. "Cooking didn't move me but drink mixing...Let's say, I finally felt something. A passion of a sort." He smirked. "A passion I'd have never met, if I had run away."

Rize caught a whiff of the flavoured air, and her heart skipped a beat. A light bouquet of fruity, ripened currant berries teased her nose. That scent ignited the vivid memories of wild Lalu'Edian forests, floral glades, and honeyed spices. Confused, she focused her gaze at the glasses.

They exhaled tart and lush. She could see a vision of grape leaves wrapped over finely chopped apples, steeped in sugar syrup, along with a generous sprinkle of roasted walnuts on the top. The treat she could taste only at one tavern in the Solar Quarter.

She hid a sad smile. Those were Lalu'Edian drinks. The mixture of pungent basil accompanied by the sweetness of currant berries distracted her from grim thoughts.

"Invigorating Currant for you," Chour gave her the glass of dark, fizzing juice, topped with crushed ice and fresh basil leaves. "Milky Mint for our nervous friend. Citrus Morning with apple slices for me...Holy elements, I need it."

"Smells like home," Rize said, barely holding in a giggle. "Cheers."

"Forget saying 'cheers' unless air meets the bottom!" Chour pointed at one of his colourful posters.

She took a sip. A tart-sweet explosion on her tongue eclipsed the darkness that had recently stormed her mood. Admitting that her neighbour indeed was a master of his craft, she chugged half of her drink in one go.

"Now listen to me," he said, amused. "It's okay to doubt, especially if you're on the verge of something new. When you feel out of place and want to give up everything you've achieved, it's okay to question if you're doing the right thing. It's mandatory for a thinking creature, to be honest."

"It's nice of you to say that I'm a thinking person," Rize retorted.

"Well..." He scratched the back of his head and laughed. "You're almost there."

She frowned. "Thanks."

"Trust me, I get it," he said. "You want to go back, where everything is *so-o-o-o* familiar that you can't help but puke. It's safer, right? More stable? Maybe. However, you're here now."

"And?"

"And fulfilling momentary whims is wrong, for there'll be no opportunity to return," he stressed his last words. "Have you thought this through? What's your back up plan?"

Chour's words worked like a choking grip. Her throat tensed. Rize gave in to the suffocating sobbing again. Her skin had already been burning from the salty tears she had shed, making it unbearable to feel anything but pain and sorrow.

"I don't know what to do," she mumbled as Amethyst put his huge head onto her lap, purring softly. "You know, we've always wanted to be our own people, independent from the Council and the overall culture that my civilisation instilled through centuries, and now—"

"You feel like you're drowning in the freedom you gained after your people had perished under piles of ash."

Speechless, Rize lifted her misty eyes. Those words hit her in the stomach, twisting everything inside. For a moment, she felt like Chour knew her better than anyone. The very thought seemed alluring. Even she couldn't put the emotions she had into one simple phrase while he did it as easily as an annoying, mundane chore.

"I feel you," he said gently, paying no attention to her baffled gawking. "You're scared."

"Of you? Yeah. Petrified, I'd say," she retorted. "How did you find out about the attack in Ponktian?"

"Not from Rel," Chour assured her. "Though, he must've told me."

"Then who was your source?" Amethyst said.

"People travel, see things," he shrugged. "They hear even more. Most people are adamant that the Lalu'Edians had too much fun with the fireworks. You know, you fired away and burned the city. The folk blame you and your...*traditions*."

"So, a hearsay?" the cat pinned down his boasting. "How prudent."

"That's not what's happened," Rize said, shocked. "No fireworks could do that."

"Guess I'm lucky to live with someone who will tell me the real story," Chour said, his smirk turned into a predatory grin. "Both of you were there. Did you see everything with your own eyes? How did it start?"

Sipping her drink, Rize remained quiet. They saw the ruins, the grand outcome, but not the attack itself. What was the Ponktian fire, after all?

That awkward silence became the personal fanfare for her stripped soul, and Chour played with it like a cat with a mouse. He could lift spirits with a jest of kindness and kill them with nothing but words. Frankly, it wouldn't be a shock to her if he used to torture people.

She examined him closely. *Is it one of his tests again?*

"You're toxic," Rize said, her voice full of disgust.

"People rarely see that because I surround myself with alcohol, which is deadly poisonous compared to me." He laughed, clearly enjoying the outcome of the game he had set.

"It looked like fire, it smelled unnatural, and it has never been discussed since," Amethyst said. "Who would believe that they bombarded themselves with fire? For what? The World's attention?"

Chour crossed his arms, his smile victorious.

"Listen," he said. "Few people have a chance to plunge headlong into adventures, especially at the Academy grounds. You don't like it here?" — he pointed at Rize and Amethyst — "Fine! Change things. Explore. Write your story. Make any choice."

"Oh, really? Just like that?" she snapped.

"You're *free*, Risotto. No family, no friends, no home, no past. Nothing. Your life now is pristine clean, don't you get it?" Chour threw his hands, getting angry. "Rel gifted you a new beginning. Clearly, he's moulding you into something. Even if it seems senseless now, trust me, there's a rational explanation and a proper outcome for everything. Even Rel's whims."

"Have you noticed how often he says, 'trust me'?" Amethyst seemed immune to Chour's charms. "Suspicious."

Rize twirled the glass in her hands, watching as the drops of her drink slid down the transparent surface. Trapped between two flames, she had to make a choice that would split and transform her life forever. It would be much easier if it didn't feel like she was standing at the edge of a cliff before the life-staking jump.

"I guess I understand what you mean," Rize muttered. "The truth doesn't matter anymore. I can't change something I don't control. Innocent people are gone, and I am here, though I don't feel like I deserve it."

"What?"

"To live," she spat. "They were people with happiness in their souls. I am just a depressed sack of meat, and I didn't ask to be alive. Life is terrible. Most people don't see that. They live in a dream, in the imaginary world created by the Council, and they *truly* love it here."

"That is a lot to unpack," Chour drawled, then added hastily. "My opinion, if I may. Until Rel starts chasing after you with a filthy broom, hold on tight with all your might to him. *Use* him, because he uses everyone. You are here because he needs something from you. It'll be a fair trade. Study, train, read, meet people, make contacts. Explore! You'll never know which day will be the last at this place. Why linger and pity your ego when you can make history?"

Those words were heavy to carry. Rize needed time to place them in her heart and mind. Her cup had already been full. Lalu'Ed zealously nurtured its children, making it impossible to broaden their horizons.

She frowned, her fingers tapping a soothing rhythm on her glass. The current reality scared her. The new system of values terrified her even more. She should've stopped dragging her old customs with her if she wanted to find home in the Academy system. She needed to adapt at least for a while to survive.

Social mimicry has never been my strongest skill, she sighed, her cheeks red after the waterfall of tears. *I must evolve.*

"I'm sick of your lectures, bipedal," Amethyst said, distracting her from the dark thoughts. "Stop prattling."

Lazily, the cat turned over onto his back and stretched out on the floor. His belly exposed, he stared at the ceiling and began to drool.

"Hey, you know what?" he looked at Chour, shocked.

"What?"

"This catnip mint is good...*meow-meowrr-murrrr...*"

Amethyst's gentle trilling swiftly turned into a heart-warming purr, making Rize laugh. She'd never seen her pet drunk.

"I went too far with the dosage," Chour frowned, his eyes sorry. "He's wasted."

His paws up, Amethyst rolled sideways, trying to catch his tail.

"Let him *explore!*" Rize mimicked his voice. "And thanks for what you said. I needed it."

The cat turned over the empty bowl from which he had lapped his milk earlier, sniffed it and froze, hunting.

"No worries," Chour said, watching Amethyst with a hint of regret in his eyes. "Speaking of desire to die, how do you like Rel's fighters?"

"Dunno," she shrugged. "I haven't met them. Why?"

"Didn't you train with them?" Chour raised his eyebrows. "Where have you been?"

"She-e-e slept and so-o-obed, ignored the ru-u-ules," Amethyst chanted, rolling over the floor again.

"I missed a training today," Rize confessed, though it was hard to feel sorry about it while Amethyst performed his next song. "Rel's off duty. He told me to stay out of trouble, so I remained here. Just in case."

"Well, the summer is ending. Even our mighty Advisor needs a day off," Chour admitted.

"In the rocky mounta-a-ains of Tsaa-a-a-an," Amethyst sang.

"Oh, really?" Chour squinted, a spark of curiosity flashed in his eyes. "Why Tsaan?"

"Don't bother," Rize distracted him. "You see that he's out of his mind."

Chour bit his lip as if pondering whether he should leave Amethyst be.

"No pressure, but you should go to the arena tomorrow," he changed the subject. "Rel's squad is here. They arrived all at once and dropped by my pub. I heard them discussing the next gathering, scheduled for the morning."

Rize gulped. *I'm not ready.*

"If I were you, I'd make up for lost time today, so that tomorrow embarrassing yourself won't be so painful," Chour said. "Don't worry about Amethyst. I'll look after him."

"Mo-o-ore mint! To the a-a-alters of mint!" the cat preached.

"I like him better this way," Chour sat by Rize, his arm wrapped around her back in a delicate hug. Embracing the moment, he put his head on her shoulder as if they were exhausted parents, watching their baby fall asleep.

Rize sighed patiently, her body stiff as a tree.

Mimicry, mimicry, mimicry...

"If you want," he whispered, "I can give Amethyst one leaf a day, so he'll stop being a brute to you and everybody else."

"It's helpful to have a brute by your side," Rize said, escaping his arm. "He always finds catty words to shut others up, unlike me."

"As you wish." Chour shrugged. "My purpose is to offer and to serve. If you change your mind, let me know. I have a bag of premium catnip soaked in poppy milk."

"Chooo', my bipeda' man…" Amethyst drawled, his tongue too numb to pronounce each word well. "Have ya eva noticed tha yar bed is on tha ceiling?"

"I have," he played along. "Extremely uncomfortable to sleep there, you know. The blanket's always falling off."

"Tha'. Is. Wron'." Amethyst dropped his head on the floor. His breath got slower, and a quiet snort resonated across the room.

Rize stepped over her pet's furry belly and grimaced apologetically, "Sorry."

"I didn't get enough rest anyway, so we'll have a great time," Chour assured her. "Go."

A contagious yawn echoed across the room as Rize stepped over the threshold. She glanced back. Chour fell on his bed and began snoring in unison with the giant black cat in the most peaceful melody two voices could've tuned.

Chapter 6
NOT AGAIN

Rize glanced up, eyes full of distrust. Fluffy clouds covered the sky; they would've seemed innocent if not for the stormy wind they brought, getting ready for the rain. By the time she finished the first lap at the stadium, a cold drizzle started tapping her shoulders and head.

Familiar, ongoing pain wrapped her muscles as her legs became stiff. She kept the speed and breathed evenly, distracting herself by observing the surroundings.

Oddly empty for this time of day, the stadium hid in between the alleys of majestic, emerald firs. The only company Rize had were swallows flying above, mosquitoes clinging to her body, and two couples on the bleachers who enjoyed the gentle rain.

The lovers stretched on the benches, noisily chatting, laughing, and kissing. Rize shook her head in disapproval and devoted herself to the training entirely, avoiding any thoughts that could tame her urge to train.

I can't run back home just because I feel off. Pathetic. I'm pathetic. No matter what, Rel helped me. I don't hurt people anymore by casting random lighting. He gave me a safe place and time to adapt, even though it's not his job to make my stay here comfortable. He's my custodian, not an innkeeper. Yes, he's rude, but his mockery seems beneficial, after all. He uses me? Fine. Rel's attitude burnt away my pride. Holy elements, he is good.

Finished with her run, Rize walked to the middle of the stadium, overgrown with soft grass. Having sat awkwardly on the cool ground, she shook the tension from her muscles. The flat lawn reminded her of the last day at Ponktian school. Oddly, Rize felt like it happened in another life, with a different, entirely unfamiliar

Mentor Keer. She smiled, recalling how the Great One and Rel visited her class.

He fixed me in just two months, she called to her reason. *Do you really want to quit a person who's better than all mentors and healers in Lalu'Ed?*

Admitting her foolishness, Rize hid her face in her hands for a moment.

The rain became heavier, making the tracks slippery. Continuing her training seemed like a waste of time, though she headed for parallel bars anyway. She tried to perform at least a simple L-sit but failed.

"Argh…" she cursed as her hands slid over the wet metal. "Demon take you!"

Rattling from approaching dark clouds, a faraway thunder caught her attention. She looked up and around. The luminaries hid behind the gloomy veil, the stadium benches became empty, and birds chirped no more.

"I must get back before the storm reaches me," she muttered and spat.

A crackling of dry branches forced Rize to look back, anxious. Someone was watching her, hiding amid the firs.

Rize frowned, pondering her next move. "Hey! Is…is everything okay there?"

A thin female figure in white robes stepped out. The veil, embroidered in silver, covered her head. The translucent lace fabric of a woman's peculiar attire got wet under the rain and revealed her delicate curves.

"Really?!" Rize exclaimed, watching the empress's soothsayer approach. "Not again! No! Stay away! I warn you I don't… .Argh," she groaned, jumping away.

Meeting with the wet ground, a peculiar crystal crashed on the spot where she had stood a moment ago. Its coloured shards trembled with a loud clinking, then dissolved into puffs of smoke. An eerie wall of black, impenetrable haze emerged before them, casting purple highlights.

"Still using portal seeds, huh?" Rize said, but got no response. "You're going to push me in there if I refuse to follow, right?" Getting the woman's silent nod, she rolled her eyes. "Fine. Lead the way."

As soon as Rize merged with smoke, the portal disappeared. Jumping into the unknown, she landed on a firm carpet and fell, scratching her knees and palms.

"How can you use these things?" Rize moaned, laying on the floor. "You know, Whitey, you should write next time. I'll put my armour on by your arrival."

"I recognise Rel's tone in your ranting. It's amusing how fast he got into your head. Get up now. We don't have time to respect ceremonies," a familiar voice uttered, but Rize never expected to hear it again. "I said, get up!" the Empress of Tsaan commanded, losing patience.

Rize jumped to her feet and asked, confused. "Why am I here?"

It was a deep and starry night outside. Empress Mar'Anna sat in a luxurious armchair that could fit at least three people. The chamber itself strongly resembled a giant's bedroom with the furniture too wide for one person. The air smelled of incense. Rize suppressed a cough, getting used to the scent.

Considering the rich decor, the ruler of Tsaan seemed out of place dressed in nothing but a nightgown. Even her face didn't glow with gilded paint, as it should've for each audience with mere mortals. Her long black hair was flowing down like steady streams over her strong shoulders, framing her wan face. Her gaze, sharp and haughty, pierced Rize through, blessing the young empress with stateliness and noble grandeur. Sitting in a suggestive silk nightdress, she seemed to be a creature from dreams: alluring, young, and demonically beautiful.

The moment Rize pictured herself in such a sensual ambience, her fingertips revealed a few waterdrops. She clutched her fist abruptly, trying to think about the ugliest pyjamas she had ever seen in her life.

"Very well. I see you passed the fire stage," Mar'Anna said and glanced at Rize's hand.

"Flames weren't a common issue. I used to cast lightning more often, Your Grace," she explained, surprised by the empress's comment.

"Lightning appears as a result of complex emotions, formed by two opposite energies. They meet, collapse, and then charge. Lightning can burn anything to the ground, can't it?" Mar'Anna raised her eyebrow. "Sounds like fire to me. But a bit trickier. Emotional dyads never produce simplicity, as you know."

"I...I don't," Rize stuttered.

"Hasn't Rel...?" Mar'Anna looked at her soothsayer. The Lady in White shook her head. "Of course, he hasn't. He never listens to me." The empress smirked. "Dyad is a two-part emotion. Sadness and anger create envy. Anger and joy form pride. Joy and fear are nothing but guilt, and fear and sadness are actually despair. All of them become bolts of lightning if one has no control over one's inner flow." She pierced Rize with her haughty gaze again.

"Pardon me, Your Grace, but..." Rize said, anxious. "Did you summon me for a lecture? I doubt my pride really is the topic."

"Partly, I did," Mar'Anna said, her lips quivered in a cunning grin. "You shouldn't leave the Academy."

Her brow lifted, Rize opened her mouth in utter surprise.

"For the first time in my reign, Ladies in White can see the Great One's lifeline clear," Mar'Anna looked at the soothsayer, waiting for approval. She nodded. "Your presence in this thread of reality lights the Citadel like the brightest beacon. Since you and your Worock aren't my people, I have no right to order you. So, I need a favour."

"I've already listened to your seer, and it brought me a pact with a demon," Rize retorted, finally getting the point.

"You can't deny it benefited you." Mar'Anna reached for a nightstand and took a tiny, metal ball to rub between her fingertips. "Crisis must happen so mortals can learn. Was your act of trust foolish? Yes. Did it help you leash your pride? Absolutely!" She threw the ball at Rize, making her duck down. "Face the consequences and be grateful for your lessons!"

Rize shivered. Sheer terror of the empress made her forget how to breathe.

"I might be a fool," she muttered bitterly, "but I'm not stupid to make the same mistake twice...Your Grace."

"Knowledge is a powerful weapon, don't you think?" Mar'Anna crossed one leg over the other, pondering. The cut of her sheer nightdress exposed the gentle curves of her body.

Rize's spine chilled. She gulped and turned her gaze away.

"I think imagination deserves more justice, Your Grace. Facts shackle our pool of choices, absorbing even the slightest glimpse of hope for a miracle."

"Miracles never happen. They are made," Mar'Anna spat. She clung to the armrests, losing patience. "Fool's hope is dangerous, especially if one acts blindly."

"I'm terribly sorry, Your Grace. I can't help you." Rize bowed her head. "Neither I nor my pet wants to be part of your plan for Eal Coras. I don't feel safe."

"I've never said I was talking about Eal," the empress said, tired.

Rize caught her sharp gaze. Mar'Anna's patience was running out.

"I know, you know," she said, bored. "The problem is we are not the only ones who share this knowledge. As I said, it's a weapon. You aren't obliged to wield it, but you'd better know how to handle it."

"I don't understand…" Rize said, her heartbeat reached her throat.

"The Great One dies in every thread." She narrowed her eyes. "Rel dies in every thread, except one."

"It can't be." Rize protested. Her feet got numb and the ground started swinging, but she stood still, waiting for further explanation.

"I can only deduce what your move is with the Citadel, but I beg you to stay." Mar'Anna sighed heavily.

The empress's poor acting was hard to miss. She knew more than anybody on the planet. The Lalu'Edians had mastered the art of manipulation, especially if it involved such emotions as guilt or pride.

"I have reasons to believe that Rel was betrayed by one of his fighters." Mar'Anna pursed her lips, worried. "I need you to be there when it all begins."

"What's going to happen?" Their chat had degenerated into a theatre of the absurd. "What are you asking me to do, Your Grace? Chasing well-trained academicians with my leaking hand? I'm no fighter. How can I possibly save a Great One? That's nonsense!"

"These events began years before your birth, and I…" Mar'Anna stuttered as cold fingers landed on her shoulder. The soothsayer shook her head softly, forbidding her to tell more.

"Well, the future is a fragile fabric. One thread could tear the whole veil apart."

Was this her doing? Rize feared to ask. *Am I here because of the empress's plans?*

"You've already believed my seer once and done as she'd ordered. Believe her inner eye again," the empress said. "Rel ignored my warnings," Mar'Anna shared her fake despair, her body moved awkwardly. That woman never cared for anything but her goals. "My cooperation with the Ladies in white makes him contemptuous. He has a right to be that. However, I don't want his limitation and principles to cost him his life, thereby destroying our future. I'll repeat — you'll be the first who understands when something is wrong."

Something wrong has been in my life for months now since the Blossom Feast, Rize thought, doomed.

"You'll sense it in your flow. When everything happens, you'll need to act fast. Promise me you'll use your knowledge."

"I'll try, Your Grace," Rize grunted stubbornly, bowing her head.

Leaning over, the soothsayer looked into Mar'Anna's eyes. The white veil remained untouched, covering the woman's face. Their eye contact seemed too intimate. Rize smirked. Surely, she looked the same way talking without words with Amethyst.

"She sees you can do it," the empress said, light-heartedly. "Now, one more thing. Your pet must know about our talk and remember that a traitor is lurking nearby."

The soothsayer pulled a crystal from her robe's folds, then smashed it by Rize's feet. It all happened too fast. Holding her breath, Rize watched as everything disappeared before her eyes in the cold darkness.

Chapter 7
AWAKENING THE NEW

The portal's touch felt like a kiss from death. Numb, breathless, and cold, Rize tried to open her eyes but ran into a wall that separated her mind from reality. Someone gently patted her cheeks. The heavy scent of incense finally woke her up.

A sharp pang.

Rize groaned but couldn't move a muscle. The suffocating smell pulled her out of oblivion. The world came alive, rain dribbling into the puddles by her ears. She clenched her jaw, desperate to remember how to see again. The bitter scent tickled her nose as someone's soft hand caressed her neck.

"She's good, *nie*?" a woman lamented. "Open your eyes, Little Flower."

Nie? It means 'no' in... Rize's heart skipped a beat. *Was that a Tribal tongue?!*

A deep, velvet voice kept talking. It dragged her out to the light where feelings made sense.

The muddy water bathed Rize's clothes. The cold ground chuffed as she moved her head. The chilling raindrops stung her, running down her cheeks. She hungrily breathed in the humid air as her spine arched in a sudden seizure.

"Ha-ha! Good-good. Don't rush," the woman said, victorious.

Rize coughed, turning over in a shallow puddle. Everything was a blur, though looked familiar. The firs behind her creaked under the stormy wind as if reaching their branches to comfort her.

They could've ported me to my dorm instead of the stadium, Rize grimaced, recognising the place.

Confused and weak, she tried to focus on her numb limbs. Little by little the sensations came back. She jerked her wrist to shake off the sticky mud and looked up, her eyes sharp.

"Who are you?" Rize said.

Another wave of coughing silenced the reply. Tasting sand on her tongue, Rize spat brownish saliva and cringed in disgust.

"O-oph, Angie! Look…Is this blood?" the other woman exclaimed, adding a fruity curse in Tribal. "I think she hit her head pretty badly."

Rize's shoulders went up to her ears as Angie touched her head. A flash of stinging pain made the stranger hiss with Rize in unison.

"I felt that." Angie grimaced and raised her hands. "Don't be frightened. I'm a healer."

Rize stared as if charmed. Angie had surprisingly long fingers. Rize imagined how easily she could fit her head in one of those hands.

The muffled voice dragged her back to reality again.

"Would you let me help you?" the healer asked louder.

"No," Rize slapped her reaching hand out of habit.

The woman tilted her head, then nodded with grace and patience.

"Lalu'Edian, huh?" she said. "You're bleeding, Little Flower."

Finally, Rize managed to focus her eyes on her saviours. The women's arms glistened in the pouring rain. They sat still like statues carved out of solid umber marble. Colourful dots of make-up formed shapes and waves, framing their high foreheads, right eyebrows, and cheeks.

Losing her last drop of manners, Rize gawked at them, unable to look away.

"Like what you see, *nie*?" one of them said. Her smile could calm the wildest storms. "Stop gaping unless you buy us dinner."

"Sorry," Rize blinked twice. "I...I..."

"Do you remember your name, Little Flower?" the healer said.

The awkward pause lingered for a while. Rize furrowed her brow, trying to recall the right answer.

"Rize?" she said, unsure. "With a Z."

"What were you doing, Rize with a Z?" Angie cast a spell, then covered her patient's head. "Training under the raging storm?"

My head fits perfectly in her hand...

"Rize?" The healer looked worried.

"Sorry. Again. Sorry," she bubbled as the warmth of healing energy wrapped her head. "That was a rookie mistake."

"Aren't you too old for a recruit?" The healer raised her eyebrow, making the colourful dots on her face sway in surprise.

"Tell this to my custodian," Rize grunted and flexed her neck. "Wow...Feels amazing. You're a good healer."

"Ha-ha," her friend slapped her hip in amusement. "You hear that, Angie? You're *go-o-o-od*."

"Obviously she's new here," she said, holding back a mocking smile. "Get up, Rize. We'll see you off to your place."

After a short walk, Rize thanked her saviours once again at the dormitory gate before leaving. She couldn't tell whether the empress summoned her for real, or she just fell and hit her head. Her mind clouded, she entered the narrow hallway of her flat, then slammed the door. It shut louder than she intended, making a clanky kettle fall from its place.

Annoyed, Rize prepared to be dramatic about it, but a burst of laughter held her back.

Amethyst, Chour, and fun? Hm...

Clearly, they had been awake long chatting and cracking ridiculous jokes. This might've struck Rize as odd, but the day's oddity limit had already been reached.

"Risotto? Is that you?" Chour shouted. "I have no desire to share with anybody but you!"

"It's me," she smiled.

Exhausted, Rize took off her shoes and leaned against the wall. The dirt on her clothes became a thin crust and started falling off in chunks. She grumbled, examining herself closely. The dusty layer of dry mud tightened her skin, making it itchy. She shivered as chills ran up her body like a wild horde.

"What is it that you can share?" Rize said. "Smells amazing, by the way."

Glancing into Chour's bedroom, her face changed drastically after seeing an unattractive-looking goop. The thick liquid of a reddish-brown colour gurgled and chuffed in a tall saucepan, producing fragrant, popping bubbles.

"I know, I know," Chour drawled, noticing the signs of disgust on her face. "It looks horrid, but trust me, you'll love it."

"What is it anyway? Beans and..." Rize sniffed, then bent over the saucepan.

"Minced meat, onions, tomatoes, and my signature seasoning," Chour boasted while the goop thickened. He threw a pinch of red powder into the gurgling slurry like a messy painter spills colours onto a canvas. "No dirty people at the table, Rize. You look like a pig and smell even worse. This odour spoils the bouquet of my culinary masterpiece." He pinched his nose, then added nasally, "Never knew Western women smelled so bad..."

The silence hung in the air, disturbed only by popping bubbles. Rize raised her elbow and marked the doorway, her armpit rubbing the wood. She said nothing as her lips froze in a vengeful smile.

Convulsing as if poisoned, Amethyst fell to the floor and spit his tongue out.

"Ugh," Chour exhaled. "You're disgusting."

"I'll never beat you at that...hey!" She lingered before their bathroom. "What's happened to the lock?"

Chour and Amethyst looked out of the room carefully.

"Well..." her roommate drawled. "We might've encountered a catnip monster."

"He broke it, not me," Amethyst snitched his partner in crime, watching Rize's attempts to close the bathroom door, but it kept opening wide with a woeful creak.

"Don't be a grouch." Chour waved off her furious glare. "There's a curtain in the shower. See? Use it!"

"Oh, really?!" Rize pinned him to the spot, her eyes spitting fire.

"Yeah. You can slide it, you know...back and forth." Chour gestured carelessly, his face straight.

"Fix the door," she demanded. "Tomorrow."

"Okay-okay. Your mistress has a temper, Amethyst." Chour stepped back, raising his hands. "Tomorrow!" he mimicked Rize. "How can you live together?"

"With difficulty," the cat muttered.

"I heard that!" she said.

"I hope so!" Amethyst's mischievous chuckle echoed across the room.

Soon enough, Rize, Amethyst and Chour enjoyed dinner together. They sat cross-legged on the floor around the gurgling dish.

Rize moaned, her mouth full. "That's surprisingly good."

"Told-ya!" Chour sang, sending a spoon into his mouth. "The most important thing is timing. Once the butter warms up, toss finely chopped summer onions onto it, so they sizzle well together. Then flash-fry mincemeat. Reduce the heat gently..." he paused cryptically. "Then, add fleshy, fresh, juice-dripping tomatoes and three pinches of *my* dried herb mix."

"Oregano and wild anise?" Amethyst rolled his eyes. "So special."

"Add hot water!" Chour raised his finger, ignoring the cat's mockery. "Allow it to boil for at least five minutes—"

"I'm a little concerned by your timbre," Rize said.

"Cooking is an art of love and passion," he stated.

"If you can sprinkle emotions into dishes, you must be a gifted mage then," she pondered.

"There's no connection between my cooking and conjuring. Honestly," he took a deep breath, "I can't really *do* magic."

Rize's lower lip quivered. Her mouth full and cheeks plump, she stared at him, forgetting how to gulp. Chour's words made no sense. It felt like her brain cells exploded. She froze, holding an empty spoon in mid-air.

"I think you broke her, bipedal."

Chour looked at the cat, worried.

"You're probably right. Rize?" he waved his hand before her eyes. "Is anybody home?"

A loud gulp.

"I just…" she caught a breath. "Why?"

"Why what?" Chour tittered. "Why am I so dashing? Why am I so talented? Why—"

"Why are you here? At the Academy?" Rize interrupted his boasting.

"I caught the interest of a custodian who found my mixing skills useful," he said. "It's not *that* uncommon. The Academy has founded many departments strictly for scientific research, 'cause many people can't cast any spells."

"Even here? Why?"

"My custodian thinks that I'm cold-hearted and have a limited range of emotions. No emotions, no juice. Can't use magic if my inner flow is empty, right? Cooking helps me, though."

Rize looked at Chour, her eyes full of sorrow. Living without constant flashes of anger, joy, or sadness seemed like a soundless life in an empty room deprived of colours.

"I'm so sorry." She took his hand as if it could help.

Chour smirked but let her stay close.

"You shouldn't be. I'm my own enemy, and it didn't stop me. Let's hope you'll find your courage to linger here too 'cause, seriously, we aren't so different."

"She's less pretty," Amethyst muttered. "Ouch!"

Rize elbowed the cat, then crossed her arms, thinking.

"I've never met anybody like you," she confessed after a pause. "Lalu'Edians without magic are as good as dead. They have no right for education and end up in the Lowcity…or worse. They become invisible…I wonder how many of them could've had a different life here, on this side of the World."

"That's a good lesson to you, *Mentor Keer*. No prism has one facet." Chour stirred the stew, then put some onto his plate. "There's always a different perspective."

They went quiet. Rize pushed the remaining beans over her plate with the spoon as something warm enveloped her chest. That was a new feeling, unknown and so fragile that it stole her breath for a while.

Did I just make a friend? She frowned.

"Stop playing with your food." Chour took away her plate. "If you want more, just say it."

Afraid to spoil the moment they'd had, she mumbled something gibberish, then giggled nervously, rubbing her neck.

"Ri-i-ight." Amethyst squinted. "When will your shift start, Chour?" He changed the subject, saving his mistress from the embarrassment.

"Thank the Universe, I'm staying home this night. Have a big day tomorrow," he said anxiously. "You should rest too. Rel's squad is…something."

Chapter 8
THE GECKOS

"Chour isn't here." Amethyst stared at the closed door, hidden in the dark of the unlit hallway. "Haven't heard him leaving. You?"

Rize shrugged.

"Maybe he finally learned how to be quiet."

With a lightened heart and spring in her step, Rize didn't walk; she almost glided to the hallway as if she was using a hoverboard. She entered Chour's room to check if he had truly gone.

Unlocked and empty, it had no signs of life except for the thick stench of yesterday's meat stew. Rize gagged and leaned against the wall. The stale air got rotten overnight, making it almost impossible to breathe in the sour odour without vomiting.

Covering her nose and mouth, Rize looked around to spot what had caused the flourishing biohazard. Her eyes down, she found a partly wet paper bag cramped and forgotten under the table.

Her moves cautious, she waved her wrist to cast a simple levitation spell. The nasty bag lifted from the floor with a gross chomping sound, blood dripping from its paper wrinkles.

"I'm not cleaning that," she said, coughing.

"It's either you, or it destroys our flat." Amethyst took a step back and shook his head, fighting the urge to breathe. "Burn it or something."

A tingling on her fingertips, Rize put all her disgust into the spell. The pulsating energy travelled across her inner flow and reached the palm at the exact moment to form a little flame. A satisfied grin appeared on her face. She looked over her shoulder.

"Cool, huh?" she said, watching as the flame's glowing tongues licked her fingers.

Amethyst purred, closing his eyes.

"I'm somewhat proud of you," he said as her spell burnt the bag to ash. "Can we go now? We're getting late."

***

The courtyard of the arena looked like a tiny square with two entrances. Each of them led to changing rooms and bleachers. Rize paced along smooth, stone tiles with Amethyst by her side, trying to spot anybody who would welcome them to the squad.

"Should we feel offended by the fact that nobody's going to introduce us to the crowd?" she said, getting nervous.

"Did you *really* expect Rel would hold your hand?" Amethyst said.

They laughed.

The ever-flowering magnolia tree waved its branches in the breeze, greeting the morning visitors. Rize stroked its pink petals, her fingers running through the young twigs, and smiled.

Soon, they approached the changing room and stopped, hearing voices behind the door. Rize's arm stayed in mid-air as her heart sank down under the sudden wave of sheer terror. She hesitated before the door, and the playful mood disappeared the moment she grabbed the cold, metal knob.

The echoing voices debated passionately on the other side. Amethyst turned his ear to eavesdrop. Nervous, Rize looked down and their eyes met.

"What's on your mind?" Amethyst asked.

Rize pursed her lips. It didn't feel right to tell him about Mar'Anna and her warning now. The day began well. Spoiling it with conspiracies and traitors seemed like a foul idea. She had plenty of time to examine Rel's squad and share her ideas after.

"Nothing," Rize lied. "Just feeling shy."

"Open up," Amethyst poked her.

Rize yanked the door and let her pet go inside first. The low ceiling along with the dim morning light made the changing room look like a dungeon with the outmost oppressive ambience.

"I still need to rehearse today. Hope Rel won't lecture us long," a female voice lamented, hidden in the shadows.

"Who is this?" the other woman said, ignoring her companion.

The moment Rize and Amethyst went down the stairs, the conversation ended. They stood at the entrance, unsure of what to say. Clearly nobody waited for them, and the awkward silence had never been handy at breaking the ice.

Finally, a red-haired woman stepped into the light. She frowned, unimpressed, while her eyes glistened like a hundred sharp blades. She hastily tousled her hair, but it instantly fell back into a short asymmetrical haircut, making Rize smirk.

Seeing that, the woman pursed her lips impatiently. It was hard to say what annoyed her the most.

"Need any help?" she said.

"We—" Rize muttered.

"Are you lost or something?" the redhead cut her off. "The Geckos booked the arena for this week. I don't know you, so..." she gestured them to leave.

"Say something," Amethyst created a telepathic bond.

"Like what?!" Rize looked down. *"Sorry, is Rel home?"*

"Call him 'daddy' instead. It would be hilarious."

"Amethyst!"

"She already thinks that you're slow. Let's have some fun at least."

Rize lifted her gaze to meet nothing but a cold stare.

"Well?" the woman spat, her hands on her narrow hips. "For Universe's sake..." She took a deep breath, but it gave her no peace. "Do you speak Global?"

"Sara, at least *try* to be nice," the female velvety voice spoke from the shadows. "It cost you no money."

"I should start charging rookies for stupidity."

The redhead granted them a crooked smile, revealing a thin scar that ran across her lips and pointy chin. She seemed otherworldly, not to mention that her green eyes glistened a bit brighter than natural.

Are they glowing? Nope. Say something normal.

"Hello…Um…Sara, right?" Rize's throat dried, getting silence as an answer. "We aren't lost."

"The Geckos must be Rel's squad," Amethyst joined the conversation, saving his mistress. "Rize, let's take a seat and wait."

"Rize?" The other woman came to the light. "With a Z?" she said, giving a short chuckle. "How is your head?"

"Oh, hi! It's good as new," Rize replied, recognised her saviour. "Thanks again."

His eyes wide, Amethyst looked up at Rize as though ready to kill her.

"Care to explain?"

"I was going to tell you," she said out loud. "Sooner or later."

Amethyst snorted but said nothing.

"It's Angie, right?" Rize addressed the healer that had helped her before.

"Angenia," she smiled softly. "You can call me Angie, of course. And this lovely girl is Sara."

"Nice to meet you," she deadpanned, manifesting the opposite. "Well, tell me who you are, *Rice*, and with what people eat you."

Sara lay down on the couch, her feet on its cushions. The others took their seats on a wooden bench across from her. Amethyst snorted, seeing how the unpleasant red-haired person occupied the whole couch. Her smile snide, Sara granted him a mocking look.

"Oh, this one's shady..." the cat thought, making his mistress nervous.

"We came to the Academy this summer. Rel gave me a pre-training course. Then, Grant joined us to supervise Amethyst." Rize briefly introduced her pet, doubting she must tell more. "Now we are here, awaiting further training."

Sara seemed disinterested in the newcomers and showed it in every possible way. Staring at the ceiling, she gave no reaction when Rize finished her story.

"I'm sure," Angie put away her long dreadlocks, tying them into a knot, "Rel will explain everything."

"He'd better," Sara grunted and sat up with a look like someone forced her to be there. "Pre-training course..." She erupted with hissing laughter.

Disappointment in her eyes, Angie shook her head but said nothing.

"How do you find Academy Town?" she addressed Rize instead.

"Unusual," Rize muttered. The unwelcoming ambience seemed wrong for chit-chatting. "I had little time to explore the surroundings, but what I saw fascinated me."

"Listen to her vocabulary, Angie. 'Fascinated'. What's next? She's gonna spice us with 'Utterly splendid?'" Sara said. "Looks like Rel dragged her from some institution of noblewomen."

"Good. Some of us need to improve their manners, *nie*?" Angie smirked, seeing Sara's wry smile fade, then turned back to Rize. "Remind me, where are you from?"

"Ponktian. It's in Lalu'Ed," Amethyst joined the conversation.

Angie widened her eyes in surprise and bowed her head, "I respect your trust to speak to me."

"Seriously?" Sara winced.

"If Rel thinks they fit, they are with us now," Angie cut her off. "You were new to the squad once. Should I remind you of that?"

"I'm a completely different package," she fumed. "The Lalu'Edians only drink, dance, and meditate."

"We are special, bipedal," Amethyst retorted, cold and protective.

Her lips quivered, though Sara held herself back. "Yeah, right…" she whispered, and a mocking grin emerged on her face again. "I suppose you miss your home. I heard Lalu'Ed is green, full of flowers and—"

"Yes," Rize tittered. "Green trees, green water, green domes. I'm afraid I'm still getting used to this land. It's too grey for me," she said jokingly.

"You should visit the Academy Gardens then," Angie said. "It's just by the temple where I serve. Hydrangeas are marvellous at this time of year."

"Angie doesn't get sarcasm." Sara sighed. "I guess it's one more thing you'll need to get used to."

Angie ignored her words.

"Amethyst, is it?" she said. "We have a Worock cat in our squad, you know."

"Rel never mentioned that!" Rize felt betrayed. "I'd love to see someone besides Amethyst. He was the only Worock in Ponktian."

"In Lalu'Ed, dearie," Amethyst corrected her.

"Can't say there're many of them here too," Angie shrugged. "But when Mars comes, h—"

"And Mars is…?" Rize raised a brow.

"A fine man. I'll ask him to show you everything that may be of interest to the Worocks. Groomers, treats, parks—"

"Of course, you will," Sara muttered from the shadows and sighed heavier than before.

"Don't mind her." Angie waved her hand. "This flower is moody today."

The front door opened, rattling as if it was kicked. Chatting merrily, several people entered the room. The last person tried to stick something between the hinges, so the door remained open, but it hit his face instead.

"It's my usual mood, Angie," Sara said after having a good laugh. "If you see me dazzling people with a smile, then I'm out of my mind."

"So...Every Friday?" The healer chuckled.

"And Saturday. And Sunday. Especially in the evenings!" the unlucky man exclaimed, still struggling with the door hinges.

"Alone…" added a tanned Tsaanish man as he collapsed on the couch next to Sara.

"In a pub…" the third continued the game.

"With a pint!" a cheeky looking blonde thundered, her fists up.

The room sank in laughter. Sara nudged the Tsaanish man with her elbow. He contrived to catch her hand. Playfully, they competed in grips until the redhead gave up, finding herself in his arms.

Rize cringed inside but showed nothing. The permissible boundaries of social interaction were strictly observed in Lalu'Ed. Even innocent handholding, not to mention hugging in public, was considered immoral and disrespectful towards others. One could end up detained for breaking those rules.

Feeling sick, Rize looked away. She examined the others' reaction and copied their smiles to blend in. Amethyst chuckled, seeing her grimace.

"I warned you, Sara!" The man finally dealt with the door and joined them. "Your solo outings wouldn't go unnoticed. Hey, Risotto," he nodded with a smug grin.

It was Chour.

Startled, Rize and Amethyst gawked at their neighbour, unable to nod back.

"I like to sit alone, okay?" Sara said. "Stop making me a bad person, Chour. You know that I drink nothing but pomegranate juice."

"As bitter as yourself," the Tsaanish whispered to her ear, throwing his hand over her shoulders.

"Knock it off, Bram," she burst out.

Resisting his advances, Sara swung to hit the man. It seemed like he gladly allowed her to get even this time, not forgetting to hug the redhead roughly after she finished punching his chest. Eventually, Sara stayed in Bram's arms, letting him caress her shoulder.

"Why didn't you tell me?" Rize looked at Chour while everyone was distracted by the fight.

He sat down next Rize and Amethyst.

"How could I deprive you of a deliciously exciting morning?" Chour said, watching Sara trying to bite Bram's hand. "Did you enjoy it?"

"We were thrilled, bipedal," Amethyst deadpanned.

"Not again! I thought we passed that 'bipedal' stage in our relationship," he said.

"Trick us more often and see where it brings you," the cat warned him.

Amethyst's last words drowned in cheering roars. The lovers' dispute turned into a show again.

"I thought only graduates were taken into the Citadel squads," Rize lifted her eyebrow, hinting that Chour's presence surprised her.

"True…But you're not a graduate either," he shrugged. "We are exceptions, 'cause we're incredibly talented. Moreover! You didn't think we lived together by coincidence, did you?"

"Rel said it was necessary. Knowing him, I dropped any further questions," Rize said.

"Wise," Chour praised her. "Soon you'll see that Rel has a thing for unusual…or shall I say, *broken* people," he whispered, his voice mysterious.

"Really? Why?"

"Maybe he can't fix himself and helping us brings him moments of short peace." Chour tilted his head playfully. "What could distract better than other people's problems when we're too afraid to face our own?"

A wrinkle touched Rize's forehead. She said nothing, pondering if Chour deduced Rel's reasons from the pub gossip or knew him for real. She shifted her gaze, choosing to remain silent.

Angie observed Sara and Bram this whole time. Her round eyes mirrored fret thoughts, visible to anyone who noticed her stiff posture. Tired of the scene, the healer looked away.

"You've already managed to establish connections, I see," Angie said, pointing at the young man. "Chour is the most sociable of us."

"What can I say? People are drawn to me," he murmured and straightened his shirt, smiling enigmatically. "They are butterflies, and I'm their sweetest nectar."

"I missed you, my dear," she cooed.

Angie blew him a kiss and giggled when he caught it. It seemed theatrical but it was *their* game. Rize sensed the warming spirit they shared. It was a soft, caressing touch of a longing emotion that slid over her shoulders and head. She had never experienced such energy herself and couldn't get why she smiled and felt it now, sitting between the two healers.

"They are connected...somehow," Amethyst thought into her head, sharing her confusion.

"How do you know?"

"I can see it," he said, concerned. *"It was barely visible before they all came. Now, it's like an endless crossroads of something swirling and...dusty."*

Troubled, Rize rubbed her temple. The room seemed overcrowded, though there were less than a dozen people inside. The buzzing noise drilled her skull. She inhaled, getting used to the surrounding bustle.

"How was your summer?" Angie asked after a pause. "Tell me you were a good boy, *nie*?"

"I had no rest. Moreover! I've been having an op all this time." Chour glanced at Rize and Amethyst conspiratorially. "And you? You look tired."

"Oh, I'm good, thank you," she said, her eyes sparkled joyfully.

Rize sensed her pendant heat up under her shirt. It felt safe and warm, somehow soothing all the troubling thoughts she had. Suspicious, she glanced at Angie and tried to resist that sedative aura. The calming tone of her velvety voice streamed like a restful spring, sowing kindness and courtesy. Her every word carried a pacifying energy of care.

"I managed to make the pilgrimage I told you about last year. It changed my spirit," Angie added secretly.

"Angie is something like a spiritual patron in the squad — cures wounds, heals minds, supports our spirits," Chour explained, which immensely helped Rize to overcome her conflicting feelings about her. "Well? May I finally congratulate you, my friend?"

"You may," Angie said as the others went quiet, listening to her. "Now I'm officially recognised as a priestess in the Temple of Elements. Once a week, I hold a singing prayer for parishioners. I must rehearse with the choir daily, but it's a nice repose after workdays."

A slow sequence of claps ran across the room.

Everybody turned their heads back to see a man giving a lazy ovation by the entrance.

"I always envied your devotion to service. Well done, Angie," Rel said, his voice proud. "Great news, which we'll certainly honour after the training."

Three more people entered the room. Rel, and a tall, young man with his Worock.

"It's smaller than I expected from a trained Worock," she thought to her pet.

Amethyst tensed as they came closer. He examined the wildcat and ignored his mistress's nudging while those present hooted and shouted in triumph.

"Today's our first meeting after the break. Therefore, I won't keep you long," Rel reassured his people when they got quiet.

"Yeah, right…" Sara muttered and pushed Bram's hand from her hip.

"You always promise us that, Rel, and then we crawl back home at sunset," Mars said, petting his Worock.

"Easy, Mars. Otherwise, he'll make a hood out of your skin. I refuse to carry you home, so behave," a sweet female voice uttered.

Rize glanced sideways, confused who had said the last words. Carefully shifting her eyes from one person to another, she turned to Amethyst for a clue. Nonetheless, her pet was too busy to notice his mistress's distress this time.

Peeking at Mars's cat, Amethyst sat quietly. Afraid to blink, desperate to look calm, he wagged his tail fretfully. Rize hid an emerging smile, covering her lips with her hand. A wild guess flashed in her mind. She realised why that Worock seemed smaller.

"It's a female," Amethyst thought, awed.

"Holy elements, you're so cute," she replied, grinning. *"Relax. You look like a furry boulder."*

"I'm starting to think that bile is in Worock blood." Rel patted Mars on his back in support. "Speaking of kittens. Rize, Amethyst, welcome to the Geckos."

"Oh." The blonde tilted her head, curious. "I didn't notice we have guests."

"Princess, you're a scout…" Rel shook his head. "How could you?"

The petite "princess" stuck out her tongue. Rel smirked as if he knew her wrinkled grimace would soon shift to a cheerful grin.

At one beat of the heart, she changed. If awakening summer had a spirit, she would be it. Her smiling eyes, blessed with mischievous sparkles, studied the strangers carefully. Little prairie suns, dipped in green fern fields, painted her irises. Those were the eyes of chirping birds, warming forests, and gentle promises at dawn.

"Rize and Amethyst are new members of our squad, Laily," Rel addressed the blonde again. "They have a lot to learn, and all of you will help me with that."

"Hm." Bram smeared Rize with a hungry stare. "Preem. Fresh. Meat."

Rize's pendant shook quietly under her shirt.

"If I were you, bipedal," Amethyst woke up from his stupor, "I would've dropped the browsing."

The cat stepped down from the bench and shielded his human, menacingly baring his fangs. A snarl trembled in his chest as Bram ignored the warning. His feline body tensed, Amethyst lowered his head, getting ready to attack.

"Wo-o-ow," Chour leaned back. "I haven't seen him like that before. Holy elements, I thought he was a harmless Lalu'Edian cat."

Angie frowned, worried. She observed the scene as if waiting for the crisis to unravel.

"Amethyst, it's fine," Rize said softly. "He didn't mean anything bad."

A traitor should be snooty, right? She thought.

"Maybe so. Maybe not," Bram scoffed as if reading her mind.

Rize's pendant clanked, which only encouraged him. Another browsing attempt followed shortly. Rize could feel his energy envelope her, poking and scratching with wiggling thorns. His spirit was rough and felt nothing like Chour's. Stoic, she pretended to care less while Bram searched for the breach.

Amethyst gave a blood-chilling hiss. The nearby humans flinched in distress, taking a baffled step back, but Bram didn't grant them attention. Rize pressed the pendant to her body to prevent it from knocking out under her clothes. It started trembling, increasing the amplitude, whilst its metal burned her palm and chest. She held it anyway.

"Stop it! Now!" Angie demanded, noticing Rize's movement. "Or you'll heal without my help next time. I swear, even Rel won't persuade me to touch you!"

It ended as fast as it started. Bram gave up, a mean grin stuck to his face. He took Sara's hand. They sat still, though their eyes mirrored a hysterical wave of suppressed laughter.

This pile of muscles afraid of a healer? Rize thought.

"Easy, I just wanted to feel her skin," the Tsaanish looked at the new member of his team. "Ya've got a sweet talisman, Risotto."

"I'm pleased my 'skin' got under yours," she said as Amethyst came back to his seat. Thanks to that minor scuffle, the cat recovered from the awestruck staring and sat relaxed in his usual cocky manner. "However, we are not here for this kind of fight. Rel?"

The corner of Rel's mouth quivered, hiding a smirk. "Priority of deeds over words guides you even now. Mentor's trait, I suppose?"

"You brought a *mentor* from Lalu'Ed?" Sara gasped with laughter. "Seriously?"

"She attacked the Great One, and she's still alive," Rel said, enjoying her astonishment. "She'll fit. Unlike many of you, Rize and Amethyst detest vain violence." He reached his hand back, clearly waiting for something to happen. "Crypt?"

Rize narrowed her eyes, noticing a shift in the shadows. A skinny hand passed Rel a glass screen. Its thin fingers slid away as the owner of the gadget stepped back.

The Geckos had one more member in the squad.

"No offence, Risotto. He doesn't like new people." Rel waved off her questioning gaze and read the first line from the screen, "The World news. Tsaan civilisation. An intruder stole a duck family from the zoo and went swimming in the nearest fountain."

Angie gritted her teeth. "Why do you and Crypt always find the most ridiculous way to end up in the news?" she said.

"It says 'an intruder', not Abram Fatherless." The Tsaanish shrugged.

"I know you bribed the reporter," Rel said. "Stop setting up the squad. We've already lost two ops because of your duck jokes."

"He started it!" Bram raised his voice in defence and pointed at the man, hidden in the shadows.

"Silence!" Rel barked. "I'm sick of you. Today you'll train with Angie."

"I'll be gentle," she whispered, and granted Bram a victorious smile.

"Itiz," Rel announced the next civilisation. "A village of clay diggers claimed that a red-haired soldier kidnapped their children for ransom. The authorities closed the case due to lack of evidence."

"The children were found…Unharmed," Sara added under Rel's piercing stare. "I took a gig, they refused to pay after I did it. The folk needed some *convincing* to find the money fast. I'm not the bad guy in this story."

"How did you escape their guards?" Rel's voice could freeze the blood in one's veins.

"I shared!" Sara giggled. "Everybody likes easy money."

"Kidnapping and corruption." He pinched his nose and sighed. "Perfect."

"Your action's getting vicious, guys," Chour muttered.

"Do you want me to tell everyone about yours, little man?" Sara cooed. Chour's face whitened. "That's what I thought."

"But he's right," Mars joined the dispute. "Systematic abuse of skills and power could ruin our career. It's not funny."

"Won't your mummy and daddy cover your smooth baby-butt in that case?" she kept mocking.

"Shut up, Sara." Laily lost her temper, and a simple "make me" in response exploded through the room. The air electrolysed under the rumble and nasty curses.

Rize, Amethyst, and Rel traded looks.

"*This* is disturbing," Rize said when he came up. "Even my nephews were less edgy at their puberty peak."

"Any suggestions, Mentor Keer?" he said sincerely humbled.

Whether it was her test or his entertainment, Rize wanted silence at any cost, and she knew the spell that seemed perfect for the occasion. She bent fingers whilst disapproval became the fuel for further conjuring. The moment magic tickled her palms, she waved her hands up and forward, summoning a gust of wind.

Watching the Geckos balancing on their feet after the spell, she jumped off her seat.

"Sorry for that. It always helped me to calm down my students." Rize gulped, pinned to the spot by many eyes. Annoyance, confusion, anger, curiosity — she received it all at once. "You needed it, trust me."

The ringing silence walked into the room, stretched its long arms, and reigned with the power to make people never speak again. Finally, Angie roared with contagious laughter, slapping her knee.

"Try this one more time and—" Sara looked at Rize, but the healer started wheezing, chuckling at her last breath.

"And nothing! You'll do nothing! Ha-ha-ha! She just," Angie caught her breath, closed eyes, and waved, "poof! You should've seen your faces. Ha-ha-ha! An innocent flower of joy!" She placed her face into her hands, trying to stop laughing. "I love her already." The muffled words came out as she began swaying back and forth.

"I'll end you at the arena," Sara said, her voice cold.

"You won't," Rel said. "Laily is your partner for today."

Sara sniffled and spat on the floor. Her body tensed and her nostrils widened. Rize wouldn't have been surprised if she began breathing out fire. Although Sara vibrated with anger, nothing happened. She demonstrated exceptional self-control.

"Rize has the same issue. She's learned to channel her emotions just recently." Rel looked at Sara patiently. "Honestly, I think new blood could give all of us food for thought," he muttered.

Sara scoffed and leaned back, annoyed.

"You'll have time to know the newbies after our training," Rel said. "Get up now. Don't trudge like sleepy moths! To the arena! Chop-chop!"

Everyone headed towards the exit obediently, saying nothing.

"This day is getting exciting," Angie whispered.

"Amethyst, Grant is waiting for you outside. Chour, work with Rize, will you?" Rel asked before they left.

"Beware, roomie." Chour gently nudged Rize. "I'm no mage but strong enough to knock you down."

"You shouldn't underestimate me either," she played along.

"Well, you have a gut of iron," he muttered. "I kept a low profile for a month before I confronted someone from the oldies."

"Because you're a coward?" Amethyst said.

"Because he hates useless fuss!" Angie pecked him on his cheek and joined their company. "That's why I love you."

"You love everybody, it's your job," Chour drawled. "Thank you anyway. Don't touch Rize, though. She's Lalu'Edian," he said, letting the ladies enter the arena first.

"Hey! I'm cool, *nie*? I know Lalu'Edian culture. Pity, but…" Angie pursed her lips for a second. "Doesn't matter. Now you're here, Little Flower. You'll fall for my hugs and kisses," she said, and walked towards Bram.

"Um…Wait. Angie!" Rize stopped her, anxious. "When you said you know our culture, did you mean—"

"Meditations, spirit consumption, childbearing. Everything," she said, then rolled her eyes, hearing Bram calling her across the arena as politely as he could.

"He's so cautious with you as if he's afraid you'll do something to him," Rize said, her voice down.

"On the contrary." Angie sighed. "He's afraid of what I *won't* do. After all, it's me who puts his guts back inside every time he messes up. If not for me, he'd have died many moons ago." She smiled smugly, her hands on her hips.

"Angie!" Bram roared, impatient. "I'm gonna get old and die while you have enough chit-chat. Let's fight!"

She laughed.

"He's ridiculous," Angie said. "Why don't you pop in to the temple tonight? I'll answer your questions after the rehearsal."

"Without me, Rize." Amethyst pricked his ears, watching the healer go away. "I hate your human temples. They stink of lavender and rotting apples."

"I bet you have other plans tonight anyway," Rize said, watching Mars's pet. The cat ran to Grant, slicing the air, and jumped right into his arms. The custodian groaned and bit her ear playfully. "Looks like they adore each other."

"Whatever…" Amethyst muttered and walked away.

Chapter 9

FRESH BLOOD

"I wonder if they get along," Chour said, watching the cats fighting under Grant's supervision. "Having two Worock cats is a boost we've been waiting for."

"Why? What's wrong with the squad?" Rize asked.

"Not with us precisely. I'd say, with all Academicians. The Geckos needed new blood to evolve." He paused, distracted by his thoughts. "Each squad has a strong leader. We are the power... I mean, you heard Rel lecturing Sara and Bram. Being an Academician grants you significant influence. It's a tempting, shady privilege that brings only harm. Trust me, I speak from experience."

"Do you want me to believe that Rel is against it?" Rize chuckled. "He controls everything that moves."

"Rel disdains power in its every manifestation: influence, knowledge, weapons, magic. The latter is the power he hates the most. That's why he makes us train our physical and mental skills. A combination of both is deadly. He teaches us to control them when other custodians drain their charges until they can walk the World no more."

"But controlling is also a power," Rize noted. "Of a dictatorial kind, I must say. You can't suppress your demonic canker forever. Eventually, it will break free."

"True. Doesn't mean I'm wrong, though. Keeping the peace is our only priority. Sometimes academicians forget that," Chour said, then nodded at the arsenal nearby. "Grab your weapons, Risotto, and stay alert if you want to remain in one piece."

"Opponents boast only if they're worth nothing," Rize teased him, picking up her daggers. "You're worried that I'm better than you."

"Oh, a kitten has claws!" he said, then cooed a greeting once his hand touched the smooth handle of his axe.

The axe was small, but its light weight helped Chour throw and swing it with minimal effort. He checked if the forged head fitted the shaft tightly and smiled. The blade's steel glimpsed in the dim morning light.

He began sharpening the weapon, enjoying Rize's curious stare. The axe sang at each stroke as if pleased to be cared for.

"You like it?" He demonstrated his weapon.

Rize nodded, charmed by its beauty. "Do the ravens mean anything?" she asked, pointing at the carved birds on each side of the blade.

A mysterious smile emerged on his face.

"They might," he said carelessly and took a defensive position. "Ready?"

"Y-yes?"

His jaw clenched, Chour advanced and raised his axe. Hesitating for a moment, Rize dodged it clumsily and pushed his back as she slid behind him. A heavy sigh escaped his chest. He frowned, defeated.

Her grip tight, Rize checked on her daggers. They were useless in today's spar unless Rel wanted them to stab each other to death. She had no chance to share that bright thought, though.

Chour took a swift sidestep, thus starting the next round. Having little time to plan her move, Rize chose a deceptive tactic. Her feet shuffled and a small cloud of dust stained her shoes when she rushed forward.

The young man smirked. Her advance looked barbaric which had its charm against arrogant fighters.

Sensing no catch, Chour swung his weapon to knock Rize off balance. She was faster. Leaning back to the ground, she slid under his arm and let the coasting save her from the hit. The trick was so childish that she could hardly believe it worked. Wasting no time, Rize jumped on her feet and trapped Chour between her blades.

"Not bad…" He paused, his skin got scratched against the blade. "…for a rookie."

Slowly, Rize put her daggers away. "Rel taught me a couple of things."

"Which makes this interesting. Let's see how fast we exhaust each other," he said, wiping a tiny drop of blood. "Ready?"

She nodded.

Chour ceased to hold himself back, and the second he had a chance for a short series of slashing attacks, he advanced. Rize parried once, twice, then again and lost one of her weapons. The axe slid down the dagger's edge and whooshed by her ear. Time slowed down as her heart skipped a beat.

"Are you crazy?!" Rize yelped, getting out of his way like a true deserter, which made the nearby Geckos laugh.

"Have mercy, Chour," Rel said when she hid behind his back. "You alright there, Risotto? Angie can heal you if you are injured."

"I'm fine," she grumbled.

"Go back to your position, then. Chop-chop," he said impatiently. "And *never again* lose your weapon."

"We were just having fun, boss," Chour said, playing with her lost dagger.

"I have no use for her if she's beheaded. Now go."

Rize followed Chour with a bit of distrust.

"We need to set some rules," she insisted.

"Alright," Chour said, pleased by the caused scene. "No slashing and no kicking each other's heads. Sound fair?"

"For now. Thanks." She sighed, tired. "Shall we try again?"

Chour took a defensive position before her. "When you're ready."

The next round could have bored them quickly if it hadn't been ridiculously comical. They circled around without any rushed strikes, having no idea how to end that light-feet courtship and flip it into a real spar. Each attack landed with a touch and a whisper of 'hit you' and then 'hit you again.' Eventually, they crossed their weapons and froze in a twisted position as if hugging. Suppressing a titter, they took a pause for a second.

"Is that a peacock mating dance?" Rel shouted, annoyed.

"You asked not to hurt her!" Chour said, and a silly smile emerged on his face.

"Oh, give me a break!" Rel fumed. "Stop fooling around and fight, for Universe's sake!"

This time they followed the order. Rize danced around Chour to exhaust him. Breathing heavily, she tried to knock him off his feet, but failed every time. Once he got lazy, she landed a satisfying punch to his ribs.

Chour riposted in no time. He thrust the head of his axe, making Rize step back. Baffled, she failed to dodge what happened next.

"Rel taught me a couple of tricks too," he said.

A condescending smirk touched Chour's lips, and a brutal kick to her torso ended the fight.

A gasp of surprise — her gasp — echoed in Rize's ears. Seeing strange black stars above, she fell back like a heavy sack and groaned. The ground rustled angrily as if offended.

"Told you I'm not that bad." Chour grinned, giving her a hand.

Rize accepted his help with a sour grimace. She picked up the fallen daggers and returned to the starting position. Catching a breath, she noticed how good the other Geckos were at fighting. Even Angie, who apologised to Bram after each victory, moved faster with a steel spear than Chour with his light axe.

"Rel had paired us for a reason, huh?" Rize muttered, still watching Angie.

"Yup. We are weak," he said, proud. "But I have other talents. Surely, you have too. Ready to try again?"

"In a moment," she uttered, parrying the thrust of his axe, and suddenly an idea hit her troubled head. She smiled, finding a great starting point for her investigation.

Too busy toying with his axe, Chour missed her cheeky grin. She smirked. She looked at a perfectly informed man who could spill all the secrets she needed. Using him, she could spot the traitor in no time.

Rize realised she must evolve to fit the new lifestyle, though it didn't mean she should leave the Lalu'Edian legacy behind. After all, the people of her nation were spectacular manipulators.

"Tell me about the Geckos," Rize said, faking awe.

"Why?" Chour chuckled, amused by her doe-eyed look.

"You're kidding, right?" she said, setting up the best trap in her arsenal. "You, guys, are amazing! I wish I could be so skilled one day. I mean," she pointed at Bram, "He's not my favourite person here, but Angie is making a meatloaf from him. A healer who can fight? That's badass!"

"Want to distract me?" Chour asked and swung at her, starting another spar.

Rize leaned to the side, then pushed him away.

"Nah," she said, breathing heavily. "Just my idle curiosity and admiration here."

"Well…" he tilted his head. "I'm from Itiz civilisation. Frankly, you know my story a bit. I told you that Rel helped me, remember?"

Rize nodded.

He pursed his lips as if choosing words. "The pub owner caught me brewing poison. By that time, I rarely visited seminars, but I had been already working as a master of drinks. I was quite well versed in herbs. Trust me, I knew what I was doing. However, my scientific interest and thirst for knowledge had no justification since it was forbidden to hang out in the kitchen outside of working hours."

Rize lunged to imitate a fight, seeing Rel's annoyed glance.

"In reality," Chour dodged, "I was checking what would happen if I mixed colchicum seeds with sumach juice. Don't want to bother you with such details as alkaloid isolation, so I can only tell you that when you brew poison, people may notice."

"Wow." Rize was speechless.

"Yeah…wow." He sighed. "I had a hearing for theft from the chemistry warehouse, deliberate harm to the community because the poisonous fumes could've killed someone and... Let me think."

Chour looked up as if the sky could help him remember.

"Right! Abuse of the staff. I asked my colleagues to cover for me."

"Really?" Rize lifted an eyebrow.

"Well, maybe I didn't ask, and instead blackmailed them."

"I live with a dangerous man," Rize muttered.

"That's why you're perfectly safe," he said. "Long story short, Rel was at the hearing as a member of the college. Everyone wanted me expelled, but Rel convinced the judge that it was necessary to strengthen the security measures for all public facilities in the Academy. He vowed there'd be no problem with me under his care. My talents had been used and managed properly since then. Now I work, study, and train with the Geckos."

Still pretending, Chour played along when Rize knocked him down with a sweep.

"Why did Rel take you into his squad?" she asked.

"He needed a herbalist," he said, laying on the ground. "Each elite squad must have two healers. Angie works with the elements and energy. I work with everything that nature provides."

"Elite squad?" Rize half-arched her eyebrow, waiting for him to get to his feet.

"Yeah, we're spies. Didn't you know?" He froze, surprised, and hesitated. "How did you get here if you know nothing?"

"Later. Keep working." Rize thrust at him furiously as Rel watched them. "Tell me about the others."

"Angie was born in Yenem," Chour said. "However, you might've guessed that—"

"Her ancestors are from the Nightmare Lands?" Rize said. "Which tribe?"

"Not the slave traders," he assured. "I know little. Angie isn't a first-generation healer. Her grandmother was like the chief cleric or something. Served her last years as an Elder in the Citadel."

"This Citadel?" Rize pointed at the towers behind her back.

Chour nodded.

"Don't let Angie's kind face confuse you; she's stronger than all of us combined." He chuckled. "She works hard to succeed her ancestor. Even wants to become an Elder too."

They watched as Angie threw Bram to the ground. At once, she dropped her spear and began examining his knees and arms. Obviously used to it, he paid no attention and kept laying meekly until she stepped away.

A sudden shuffle distracted them. Rize jumped behind Chour's back, almost getting hit.

Two fighters slashed the air as if the whole arena was their battleground. Laily dodged Sara's knife and slid forward, sweeping the ground with her barley-blonde hair. She dropped her opponent down to win time for her next lunge. The blade bounced off, leaving Sara unarmed, and a dazzling smile revealed the rose glow on Laily's cheeks. Swiftly, she threw her legs over Sara's shoulders and trapped her neck between the thighs.

"Want to try again, redhead?" she panted, then looked up at Chour and winked.

"What about the blonde?" Rize whispered.

"Barklaily Waters. Her parents believed that name was good, hah. She hates it, by the way. Some graduates of her year, who stayed at the Academy, still tease her, 'Bark, Laily! Bark!'" Chour looked at the blonde tenderly, unable to form sentences. "She's like a sister to me. Really kind. And funny. Laily studied in Monok civilisation but was born in Runv."

"Explains why she's so small and wiry," Rize said. "What's her job?"

"She's our scout. I mean… You saw how fast she is. It's a wonder. Can't be body weight alone, can it?"

"It could be if she possessed one of the *signs*. The Universe helps her, providing her with elemental force. Stealth and lightness are the main features of the air blessing."

"I confess, I've never peered under her collarbone." Chour scratched his head. "Who's next? Sara… Sara is a difficult person, but finding common ground with her is easier than it seems. Unlike Bram, she doesn't mock people for fun. I'd say she simply protects her space."

"And you're saying this beca-a-ause…" Rize squinted.

"I see right through people and know when their glasses need a refill, Risotto," he said smugly. "Angie assured me that Sara used to be much more troubled than today."

"Hah, I suppose Bram calms her down," she said.

"Honestly, I find him rather obnoxious and disapprove of his methods. Rel says that we needn't like each other. Having a common goal is enough."

"You disagree?" she asked, hearing his voice cracked.

"It's not my place to question Rel's ideals, but yes. I do." He used Rize's hesitation, advanced, slid behind her back like a dancer, and trapped her neck in a fierce chokehold. She gasped, catching air, and dropped her daggers, fighting his stiff arm. Chour's warm breath tickled her ear, "Bram dragged us out of top-rated scum when even Angie was ready to die."

"To die?!" Rize elbowed him in his stomach.

A short groan. He loosed his grip, letting her escape.

"What kind of operations do you people execute here?"

"Your hand…" Chour jerked his chin. "Do you need a break?"

Rize glanced down. Water drops lingered on her fingertips, ready to meet the ground. She fought the gnawing embarrassment and wiped her hand on her T-shirt.

"Answer the question," she said, her voice plain.

"If Rel hasn't told you yet, there's a reason." Chour came up and examined her glistening palm. "Sara ignites her skin when she's angry, you know, but this…Hm. Interesting," he muttered. "Can you tell what caused that?"

"No. It's recent. I used to stun people with the lightning. This is new." She took her hand back and massaged it carefully. "Maybe I'm just tired."

"Shall I continue your Gecko-orientation-tour to smooth this awkwardly wet situation?" Chour picked up and threw the fallen daggers back to her.

"Yeah. Tell me more about Bram."

"Rel spotted him at the Arena Games — our local sports competition. They say, it was hard to miss his glow. Bram led the standings in four out of five disciplines, was famous in certain circles, and his army of fans chanted so loud that roars and cheers could've spread throughout Academy Town. He graduated with honours from the Military department, so Rel invited him to join Sara, Laily, and Angie."

"There were no men in the squad?" Rize said, shocked.

"The team proliferated after Bram had joined. As Rel once told me, he didn't want to take typical academicians in. I mean, look around. You'll see people of all civilisations. One is an outcast, the other is a priestess. The third is a petty criminal," Chour hinted, pointing at himself. "The best graduates are trying to get into the Geckos, but Rel is hard to impress. I wonder, what's it about you he found so intriguing?"

"Chour, stop flirting! Risotto, concentrate or I'll be your opponent for the next spar!" Rel said, his hands on his hips. "And I saw that you lost your weapons. Again!"

"Ask him." Rize took her position.

Chour looked at their custodian with a hint of distrust.

"Not today," he uttered. "Rel shares his thoughts in exchange for something. I have nothing to offer him yet."

"You have stories for me, though. Mars, his Worock, and that skinny man who dislikes new people." Rize dodged a sudden lunge and kicked Chour under his knee. He lost balance and fell.

"Nice one," he grunted, his face planting the ground.

Rize kneeled to check if he was alright, but Chour waved her off. He rolled to his back, panting.

"The skinny man is Crypt. I don't know his full name. It's classified like all data about Monokiese scientists. He knows everything about programming, mechanics, and understands the latest technology. He's our debugger."

"What is a 'debugger'?" Rize imagined Crypt stomping insects but doubted his occupation had something in common with nature.

"Demons…" Chour cursed, standing up. "I always forget that you're Lalu'Edian. Strange that you didn't ask, 'What is programming'?"

"Because it would take longer to explain?" Rize assumed, watching Rel fiercely lecturing Sara for smashing Laily's lip to dripping blood.

Angie rushed to the blonde to tend her injury. In a second Laily's lip was whole again.

"Probably, you're right. How can I put this?" Chour frowned. "Remember that glass screen I gave you? It's a device programmed for certain functions: reading and searching for information. Now imagine there's a device that blocks your attempts to open something. A door or…access to the information storage that you need."

"Why can't I open it? It has no handle or…?" Rize said.

"It's not because of a handle. Ugh…" He pinched his nose. "It's a lock. A lock for which you need to pick up a key. Sometimes several keys. A debugger searches and tries numerous keys to access what the Citadel wants."

"Where does he get so many keys?" Rize asked, confused. "And why should he pick them up anyway?"

"He doesn't—" Chour closed his eyes to find some peace. "Universe, have mercy on me…He doesn't have these keys. They aren't physical. Crypt has special things that are made of numbers because the locks are also made of numbers. These things pick up the keys, and Crypt controls the process."

"Made of numbers? Like El in the library?" Rize hoped she understood at least something.

"Right! But the Elevator is programmed to move people and chat. The locks are programmed to block access. Sometimes we have to gain the information that the Great One wants—" he got quiet. "You didn't hear it from me, okay? I can't explain the job better. Ask Crypt when he feels okay near you. He'll gladly tell you about all his books till you start fainting."

Rel turned his head, checking the rest of the squad. Rize flinched. Pretending to train, she knocked Chour's weapon out of his hand. The custodian snorted and looked away.

"Mars," Chour said, deftly catching his axe, "is from Yenem. His family is somehow connected with the Worocks. Either they study the cats, or breed them, or both. We joined the squad at about the same time. We even had our Dedication on the same day. I hope yours will be smoother than ours."

"What's a 'Dedication'?" Rize said.

"It's a joining ceremony when a newcomer dedicates themselves to serving. Rel altered it a bit, added some spectacular details. No more spoilers from me."

"Fine," she drawled. "So, what happened at your Dedication?"

"We got too excited and smashed a couple of faces," Chour said, looking guilty. "In fact, we were provoked, but it's a poor excuse. Adults would've gotten away from the conflict. We hadn't. And Bram...He needs little to start scattering people. He's a Tsaanish orphan! One careless word, and you'll lose your teeth."

"I'm familiar with Tsaanish temper," Rize muttered.

"Angie said that he became kinder with Sara. Hard to imagine what he'd been doing before they were together." Chour shook his head. "Anyway, he's not my business apart from his health. I prefer to hang out with Mars."

"Are you close?"

"Kinda. His cat adores me and steals catnip from my stash all the time. I, in turn, always put fresh herbs in the same place before her visit."

"What's her name?" Rize said.

"The Worock give themselves unpronounceable names. However, scientists like Mars's parents give cats labels like S-12, J-26, and so on. A letter is a month of birth, a number is an ordinal number in a pride."

"That's morbid," she said, shocked.

"It's not. The cats live in forests, move freely. No one takes them away by force or tortures them in laboratories. Scientists only observe their society, so to speak. When Mars found her, she was hurt. Her jaw was fractured, and she had that strange, drawn-out roar. She kept snarling, 'roaz, roaz, roaz'. He ended up calling her Rose."

"If, as you say, the Worocks live freely, then why did Mars take her?" Rize frowned.

"He *found* her during an expedition when his parents were looking for cat prides in other civilisations," Chour said. "Ask Mars about it someday."

Rel announced a break, rushing everyone to store their weapons.

They headed towards the exit, splitting into groups. Angie whispered something to Laily, making her giggle. They chirped about some nonsense that Rize failed to understand. Sara, Bram and Crypt waited for the custodians to join them by the door.

"Mars, hold on!" Chour saw him passing by.

In the meantime, Rose rushed away from custodian Grant. Overtaking Amethyst, she jumped on Mars's chest, making him stagger.

"Argh…You are not a kitten anymore." Mars groaned, gently putting his pet to the ground. "Oh, my back."

"Someone's in a playful mood, I see," Chour said, scratching Rose behind her ears. The cat purred, closing her eyes.

"She missed the trainings," Mars said. "I think it's all about Grant, though. Isn't it, girl? Should I worry that you'll leave me?"

Rose purred even louder and butted her master's hand, trying to hide her large muzzle in his palm.

"She's a bit shy today," Chour noticed, petting her. "Are you alright? Yesh-h-h, you are. Who ish-h the pretties-sh-t cat in the world?" he cooed gently, petting her all over the body.

"Ugh, gross," Rize heard Amethyst's words in her mind and chuckled.

"I'm Mars." The man reached for a handshake. "And this is Rose."

"Rize," she said, cautiously accepting his hand. She had been troubled by handshakes far more than usual the last few days. Thankfully, her hand remained dry. "And this is—"

"Amethyst," he introduced himself, stoically ignoring Rose.

"It's nice having you both with us," Mars said with a polite smile. "Angie asked me to show you places where the Worocks can entertain themselves and rest. At this hour, it's pointless because—"

"'Cause we must eat!" Chour exclaimed, making his way forward.

"I was going to say that everything's closed, but he's not wrong." Mars shrugged.

"Stop wasting precious time," Chour elbowed his colleagues. "I know a perfect establishment where we'll have hot brunch with a discount!"

"Is he talking about his pub?" Rize wondered.

"Yes," all the Geckos sighed in one voice.

Chapter 10
BLESSED LOOPS

Rize hesitated, lingering in the Academy Gardens. She hadn't meditated, prayed, or passed by any temples since she had left Lalu'Ed. She avoided them on purpose. No one cared about her righteous lifestyle, thus she used it as an excuse to abandon the old routine she hated so much. For a moment, this thought made her stoop like a naughty child.

Tree leaves rustled gently, murmuring songs humans would never understand. The tune soothed Rize along with the warm night, caressing her cheeks.

Is this the right place? she thought, looking at a humble building. *Oh, demons...* She pinched her nose. *Yup, it is. Where are the merchants, though?*

The temple could be mistaken for an academy department if not for the smell. The scent of lavender mixed with decaying apples suffocated anyone with sensitive noses.

Cautiously, Rize treaded forward.

The building had no guards, shining domes of gemstones, or shop-tents abundant with trinkets. There were no signs of costly candles and oils either. To a mere Lalu'Edian it seemed outrageous. After all, religion was an endless source of money for the capital. Citizens and tourists emptied their pockets at the temple daily.

Frowning, Rize looked around to check the place again. She was alone except for various nocturnal insects, partying in the gardens.

A crescendo of cicadas, sleepy but still loud, buzzed across the place. She cringed and briskly reached the temple walls, willing to hide from the mind-blowing sounds.

Stained windows, narrow and tall, kindled with warm light and promised to give shelter to all who prayed that night. Rize ascended the stone steps half-conscious, lured to the bright fire. She pulled a heavy door making it creak and quietly slipped inside.

A gentle wave of singing voices washed away the anxiety Rize had brought. She stared in awe as if charmed. Angie was hard to miss. Tall, bright, and stunning to the last thread, she winked at Rize and got back to conducting the choir.

Singing in harmonies, people rehearsed a painfully familiar prayer. The Chant of Challenge, the verses of which were never explained or questioned in Lalu'Ed. Rize remained still, chills running down her numb body.

Don't ask. Rize shivered remembering her local priestess's words. *Pray.*

The choir performed the chant much calmer than Lalu'Edians. Here, using nothing but their own murmuring voices, they filled the space with gentle music and a heart-breaking prayer. Never before had the chant to their divine stoked Rize to aching pain and misty eyes. Suddenly, she could *feel* its meaning without questions.

Distracted by the ambience, Rize failed to notice benches for parishioners. Polished dark wood glistened welcomingly in the candlelight. A tender smile emerged on her lips as she recalled the Great One, grunting in the Hall of Justice at her hearing.

That was a long time ago… Rize thought, and took the closest seat. She closed her eyes, listening.

Dissolving in bliss.

The sounds resonated with four altar bowls, walls, windows, the roof and even the floor, providing the temple a voice to sing along with its servants. If it could hug, Rize would've drowned in its embrace. She was fading, wrapped in a cloud of sheer peace.

For the first time in her life, Rize absorbed joy staying in the house of elemental deities. She felt safe, protected, and even blessed to witness the miracles of life.

The choir hummed the final chords, ending the chant. Their harmonies rose above, lingered by the ceiling, then drifted away. The last note kissed Rize's skin and gently escaped into nothingness. It felt like a cold ocean wave that tickles your toes, making every hair stand upright. She blinked. Two heavy teardrops ran down her eyelashes, slid to her chin, then her neck, and vanished behind the collar of her shirt.

The rehearsal was officially over. Angie clapped, murmuring words of gratitude. Shortly, she said her goodbyes and sent everyone away, staying alone with Rize.

"What do you say? Did you like us?" Angie took both of Rize's hands in a soft but confident grip.

"I didn't know prayers could be chanted that way." She exhaled, rubbing her nose. "Sorry, I'm a mess."

"It's okay." The healer caressed Rize's shoulders. "It means we got right into your spirit! Do you sing?"

"I mostly hum. All Lalu'Edians do," Rize shrugged and pursed her lips, regretting the awkward silence. "We are not allowed to sing or dance in temples."

"While I'm here, you can do both," Angie whispered mischievously. "Let's talk and clean up, *nie*?"

"You never rest, I see," Rize said.

"If I can help many at the same time, why avoid it?" A husky chuckle left her chest. "What questions do you have for me, Little Flower? As the Geckos' spiritual patron, I'm here to integrate you into the squad. Tell me about everything that bothers you." Angie took a mop for herself, then tossed Rize a dusting cloth.

"You said you know about Lalu'Edian culture. How come?" Rize began wiping the benches while Angie cleaned the floor.

"It was a part of my initiation. Priestesses of the elemental temple must study religious rites, customs and traditions of all civilisations. It's useful. Helps me understand people better," the healer said.

"In what way?" Rize frowned.

"We have one goddess, but you'll be surprised how differently the Universe is presented in the world." Angie sighed, her eyes lost chirpy glow. "But between you and me...the Monokiese are the worst."

"Because they prefer craft over conjuring?" she guessed.

"Because the Monok civilisation forbids prayers and any indication of us having souls. For the Archrectorate, the faith mustn't exist. They consider it heresy. Our generous Universe is just matter for them. Some even call it *space*!" Angie shook her head. "Like it's some kind of area."

"It makes no sense. The Monokiese use magic," Rize said. "Why deny its source?"

"Magic is just a tool they take for granted. Calculations, dull statistics, and reports make their world. We've recently found out they are about to enter the Universe, using a flying ship that would bring scientists to the moon."

Rize gaped at the healer. "Is that even possible?"

"Everything is possible if you focus on one goal. The only enemy you face is time. There'll never be enough of it as it consumes everything. Especially us," she uttered. "Use your time wisely while you're here, Little Flower."

"Chour says that we are our true enemies," Rize said playfully, heading to the altars.

Plugged with burning candles, four altars drowned in melting wax. Some wicks breathed out fading sparkles, cracking angrily as Rize passed by. Stone pedestals held bowls filled with sacrificed gifts.

Rize inhaled the hypnotic scent.

"Smouldering lavender is given to the air. Apples are children of the earth and manifest that decaying is a part of life. The everburning flame represents the fire that saved us from the first Darkness. Finally, the water..." Rize pursed her lips and stopped by the last bowl. "The Universe might be represented differently, but even time won't erase the elements. It has no power over them."

"You're a thinker, *nie*? No wonder Chour likes you," Angie said, still mopping the floor. "Lalu'Edians rarely oppose dogmas. Your spirit is still disrupted, but when you fix your inner flow, o-o-oph!" Her brows went up. "You'll make spells of your own."

"You can sense my spirit?" Rize tilted her head in disbelief.

"I can sense anybody's. I'm a good healer, after all. It's my job to feel others and treat their wounds," she said, her eyes flickered in a sage glimpse.

"Do you know why my hand leaks water?" Rize asked.

"Of course! You're dealing with something you've never felt before. It scares you, changes who you were."

Speechless, Rize watched Angie while she theatrically puckered her lips, evaluating the finished work. The floor tiles looked clean, so she nodded and put the mop away.

"How can I make it stop?" Rize finally found her words.

"Stop?!" Angenia gasped, insulted. "Oh, no. No-no. Embrace it. Find the root of your emotion and accept it with every fibre of your soul. It's a part of you now, so don't fight it. I know, the Lalu'Edians are taught to suppress strong feelings, but you shouldn't follow this rule here." She smiled, coming closer. "Give me your hands."

Putting away the cloth, stained with oily wax and dust, Rize placed her wrists into Angie's hands. She gently stroked Rize's pale palms and fixed her thumbs in their middle.

"Hm-m…" the healer jerked her chin up. "You're full of trust but too scared to place it into others. Even though your soul sincerely wants it. Fear is a lousy guide, Little Flower. Don't believe what it whispers into your ear."

"I like your methods better." Rize took her wrists back. "Rel said that my hand leaked because I'm in love."

"He's right."

"You just said it's because I'm afraid to trust people!"

"Pure love is a dyad of two raw emotions: trust and joy," Angie said calmly. "I suppose you have a twisted definition of love in your head. After all, your Council's propaganda claims that love is everything you do for others. A favour! An act became an emotion! They made love a trade coin, for Universe's sake!" she hissed the last words. "Love is about little things. True love comes not because *of* something or *for* something. Love is complex. You love someone out of happiness that something or someone exists. And the attitude is mutual. Comparing, judging, humiliating, betraying, arguing, fighting brings you nowhere. You hit the wall and get only bruises." Angie caught a breath, pinching her nose. "Love is a harmony of mutual acceptance."

"That's why I never understood my sister," Rize muttered after a pause. Angie replied with a silent question in her eyes. "She bears the maternal *sign*."

"Oh, right. The Mothers' cult…" Angie clicked her tongue. "Do you mean this?" She flashed her smooth belly, raising her shirt.

"I…wow." Eyes down, Rize stared at dark wavy lines that circled Angie's navel like a grapevine wreath. They bulged like scars, spoiling her shimmering skin.

"It's a mark for one of the strongest dyads — the sign of love," the healer explained.

Accepting what was said, Rize sighed and looked into Angie's deep eyes to find comfort. "Does it mean the whole sign system is based on dyads that souls can experience?" she asked.

"Indeed. I have many traits that make me a good servant, a healer, and a mage, as my energy source is a long-lasting emotion compared to, let's say, anger or shame. I'm ready to sacrifice everything, even my life, because I trust the world and find joy in easing pain, caring, and helping its children."

"I definitely have nothing of that sort in me," Rize scoffed.

"You're wrong again. You love Amethyst," Angie said. "Love has many faces. I'm sure one day someone will find your face equal to it. Love could be sweet, bitter, spicy, and even poisonous depending on the amount of trust you put into others and the joy you feed upon."

"I'm having a headache." Rize rubbed her temples. "It doesn't explain why my dysfunctional magic shifted from the lightning to water drops."

"Right," Angie nodded, hands resting on her hips. "Rel said you and Sara share one problem. Unlike her, you hopped to the next blessed loop in a matter of weeks. Interesting…"

"Has anybody told you that symbolic speeches are hard to understand if one's unfamiliar with the lore?" Rize groaned and rolled her eyes.

Angie said nothing, narrowing her eyes.

"Sorry," Rize mumbled. "I'm just tired of rediscovering everything over and over again."

"You are forgiven," Angie said calmly. "I guess you have no idea what the Chant of Challenge is about."

Rize pointed at her forehead and the corners of her mouth went down. "I'm an empty vessel."

Angie hid a chuckle.

"Blessed loops of Challenge are three life stages we all go through before we die," she explained. "Yours are physically visible because you are still learning to control the inner flow. People encounter three loops in total. Fire for loss and upheavals. Water for trials that mould your character. Brass trumpets for fame, flattery, and power…The hardest of all. Many Geckos are having it now, and I can't say they manage with dignity."

"What happens if they fail?" Rize asked.

"Life would kick them back, so the fire loop could cleanse their souls for a fresh start," Angie said. "If they complete the second stage, they would be reborn. As we come into this world from mother's waters, so the water loop brings us towards a new life."

"We come from mother's…what? I don't get this euphemism," Rize said.

"It's not that." Angie shook her head as if it helped her focus. "What do you know about childbearing in Lalu'Ed?" she asked carefully.

"Well, I'm not supposed to be interested in it unless I'm a mother," Rize mumbled. "Inni, my sister, left us for a month and came back with a bunch of babies later. I always thought the convent provides children and gives them away when it's time. You know, like a charity shop."

Angie pursed her lips, trying not to laugh, though her muffled giggling remained audible.

"I'm sorry," the healer whispered, seeing Rize's insulted eyes. "I have so many questions." She exhaled and smiled softly. "But you'll indulge me later, *nie*? Let's brush up on your knowledge for now."

"Fine," Rize grunted, her cheeks and ears flooded with burning heat.

"Frankly, our world knows two ways of childbearing: natural and artificial," Angie said. "The first is granted by our bodies and is no different to how mammals reproduce in the wilds." She made a pause, waiting, and spoke again after Rize nodded silently with a hint of distrust in her eyes. "The last is judged by many civilisations as non-humane and repressive."

"By many, but not Lalu'Ed?" Rize gave a bitter chuckle.

"And Monok. It was one of many experiments that scientists performed to prove their control over human matter. They found artificial childbearing fund-consuming, though, and dropped the idea of creating a perfect nation."

Rize placed her face into her hands.

"So, you're telling me that you crawled out of your mother like some kind of a baby bear, and I was made out of thin air?" she muttered, devastated.

"I – yes. You – not really. Babies in Lalu'Ed are made of parents'…materials." Angie chose the safest word and added, "So am I. The only difference we have is you were selected to become a particular person, and I was completely random. We all formed in the water. While I was dwelling in my mother, you had your personal bubble in the convent."

The temple sank in silence, disrupted only by crackling candles. Rize took a deep breath, trying to fit in the new information. Scented candle wax tasted sweet and pleasant, which confused Rize's feelings even more. Sweet meant good, but she could hardly feel herself okay.

"Flesh and blood," Rize recalled her sister cooing over children. She leaned back, tired, and looked at Angie. "These are materials. So, her sons and daughters have Inni in them...and I have my mother," she said, feeling sick.

"And father. More or less, you're right. I'll explain everything in detail if you want, but we need to visit the library for this. Anatomy section," Angie said. Meeting a glassy-eyed look, she tilted her head. "What troubles you?"

"I don't think I needed it," Rize confessed. "Conflict of beliefs is something that I didn't want to have on my plate right now."

"The human mind is set that way. We believe what we want to believe. That's why we have the Tsaanish, who follow vague predictions more than logical calculations and science. We have the Lalu'Edians, who ignore the basic reproductive law, hiding it behind the convent walls. We have the Monokiese, who deny recognising a soul as a living being. We have...should I continue?" Angie stopped herself.

"No-no, I got it." Rize sighed. "People can convince themselves of anything if it suits their agenda."

"And the new world that unravels before you will find its place in your heart, I promise." Angie caressed Rize's cheek. "Listen, the Universe decided that love is the emotion that could mould you better than others. Step into this experience, trusting our goddess. In order to pass the water loop, you should accept it in its many forms so you would become like water — healing, nurturing, flexible, wild, *and* bringing life. It's all connected, can't you see? Love and life are travelling together."

"You remind me of my mentor," Rize smirked. "He liked metaphors too. I bet his brain would explode if I wrote him what you told me."

"Worry about yourself in this journey," Angie uttered, her fingers running through Rize's wavy hair. "You've taught anger to be a balanced part of your essence, and it will help you with time. For now, if love is the emotion that creates you, let it guide your spirit. Talk with a person who helped you grow and move further along the loop."

"What if I don't know who it was?" Rize asked.

Angie cleared her throat, impressed.

"You've been busy, *nie*?"

Chapter 11
DREAMCATCHER
Rel

The darkness of the dream realm alleviated Rel of stress. His stiff muscles relaxed. His heart slowed. It felt like he was a boy again. His mother's hand pushed the swings where he had spent the first years of his life. It was calm. He felt safe.

Alas, Rel had no parents to remember. He was a Dreamcatcher — a bastard son born right after his mother died — which made his visions magically prophetic.

As he remembered his true nature, the vision shifted. While nothingness blinded Rel, a pitch-black void swallowed his drifting, aimless mind. He failed to resist its gentle touch. Charmed by the magnifying power, he feared what would come next. The dream that had been haunting him for months made little sense.

Something controlled his body, while Rel's troubled mind tried to wake. Finally, he bent his knees.

"Take it," a hoarse voice said, turning into a blood-chilling hiss. "Look at it. Take it. *Eat* it."

The eerie echoes filled the emptiness as if chanting a spell. Rel clasped his grip. An object, warm and heavy, emerged in his hand.

Fighting the command, Rel tried to shake his head, but it turned numb instead. His eyelids got heavy. His will ceased to exist. Forced to look down, he gave up and let the dream flow as it wanted.

"Consume," the voice whispered.

Rel stared at a human bone, resting in his hand, and his throat dried. He had seen it many times. It should've been caged and protected by multiple spells and a dozen guards, yet he held it coldly in his grip.

It's just a dream, Rel thought.

The void wrapped him tighter, depriving his consciousness of any rebellious thought.

I didn't do it.

The otherworldly power lifted Rel's arm. The artefact they'd lost, Liara's Bone, was just before his eyes. Ancient and fractured, it throbbed with a distinct beat as if it possessed life.

"Consume," the void spoke up again.

Rel brought the bone closer to his mouth and opened it. His lips cracked, getting bloody. He held the artefact like a knife and suddenly his body was *his* again. The void wanted him to swallow willingly.

Unable to fight the building hunger, Rel put the bone inside and choked, greedily forcing it down his gullet. The pain signalled him to pull away, but he couldn't stop. The rough bone ridges scratched his throat and cut his tongue, going deeper until the artefact finally disappeared.

Out of breath, Rel fell to the floor and screamed in agony. The blood burbled up in the back of his throat and spilled out of his chin. He coughed, painting his hands red.

"Finally…" the voice murmured, pleased, and its echoes dissolved into the abyss. "Now get me the diamond."

As the dream came to an end, Rel flinched in his bed with a fearful gasp. He turned to the side and fell, dragging his sheets and pillows with him.

"Argh…" Rel moaned, rubbing the shoulder he hit.

A polite knock reached his ears.

"Is everything alright in there, advisor?" the guard said. "Advisor?"

Rel stayed on the floor, hyperventilating. He swiftly palped his neck, checked his belly, and sighed. Nothing.

Every time Rel hoped the dream would kill him, but his body remained intact. No cuts. No scratches. He swiftly wiped the tiny trail of bloody saliva from his chin. The stained pillow looked horrifying, making him cringe. As the guards stormed into his chamber he turned it upside down, just in time, and prayed the Great One's hounds saw nothing.

Chapter 12
SEPARATE
Amethyst

"I'm off to the library," Rize said hastily as she dressed. She mumbled on and on, pausing and panting as if someone was chasing her, then finally went quiet.

Amethyst rested on his sofa, half-sleeping. He would've had a peaceful, scheduled nap but it was impossible with Rize in the room. The cat sighed. Last night he had to listen to his mistress's discoveries until late, which made him grumpier than ever.

"Amethyst?"

The cat jerked his tail, pretending to sleep. His mistress seemed too excited after talking with Angie, and he had no intention of supporting the mood. Religious bipedals were at the bottom of his list of brainless humans. Funnily, with all that nonsense happening with Rize, she had a solid position in his ranking and never fell below the middle.

He accidentally purred out of pleasure.

"I knew you were up!" Rize shook him. "I'll go shopping on my way back from the library. Care to join?"

His tongue out, Amethyst yawned. He stretched his paws, then closed his eyes again.

"Nah, I have plans," he said, hoping to fall asleep. "Honestly, I want our weekends to be separate from now on. I hate libraries. You are no cat. We have no future."

He held a pause, then chuckled shortly. It took humans forever to respond, though he never ceased to hope for a miracle. Bipedals were slower than any Worock by all means. Finally, Rize crossed her arms as her eyebrow twitched in surprise.

"Rose wanted to show me the Worocks' park," Amethyst explained.

"I knew there was a black cat between us." Rize squinted, playing along. "Ask Chour to close the front door after you leave. I'll come back before lunch."

"You never do," he said. "The Geckos are meeting in the pub for drinks today. Try to come back at least for that."

Rize looked at him, suspicious. "Since when did you like bipedal gatherings?"

"Since I finally have someone intelligent to talk to," he retorted, and a rumbling purr left his chest. "Rose is fascinating. I can listen to her for hours, while you…You always moan and mumble."

"Uh, I…" Rize clenched her jaw, and a short awkward pause lingered in the room. "You know, I'm glad you found a friend."

Amethyst raised his head and pierced her with a cold stare.

"Is it me, or did you just pay attention to someone else's life for the first time?" he pricked his ears, looking for a catch.

"I guess I did."

"Stop it. You're scaring me." Amethyst slid to the floor and lazily stretched his feline body. "What's wrong? Are you dying?"

She laughed, making him flinch. He had never heard *that* kind of laugh.

"No," Rize said, a silly smile stuck to her face.

"Then, did Angie do something to you?" Amethyst asked, pricking his ears. "You're weird today. I don't like it."

"It's just…" she muttered, toying with the buckles of her satchel. "I love you, and I want you to be happy."

Amethyst froze with widened eyes, his tail failed to finish a wiggle.

"Oh, dearie…You aren't weird or dying, you're simply going mad," the cat summed up.

"The Academy's playing tricks on my mind," she whispered.

"Absolutely! Look at you." Amethyst jumped on the spot, anxious. "You forgot how we work!"

"Oh?" Rize tilted her head.

"I make remarks, and you hiss at my catty jokes. Sound familiar?" he asked, worried. Confusion coursed through Amethyst's body. He felt helpless, and a heavy feeling tightened his chest. He could sense that something troubling started to unravel. "Well?" He poked her.

Making Amethyst step back, Rize kneeled, and their eyes met. She seemed sad, though the corners of her lips quivered in a gentle smile.

"Maybe it's time for us to finally grow up?" she uttered.

"Never," he said, his nose up.

Amethyst noticed her reaching hand and raised his head to meet it. Caressing his soft fur, Rize suddenly stopped and fled the room without a word. The cat jumped to his paws to follow his mistress.

Drip. Drip. Drip.

His eyes down, Amethyst was distracted. He watched as the drops of water ran down his back, dampening each hair on its way to the floor.

"Well…shit."

Chapter 13
STORIES TO BRAG ABOUT

"Ten, nine, eight…" Rize muttered. She couldn't get Amethyst's worried look out of her head. She left him confused and the scene was nothing but awkward. "Seven, six, five…"

Counting backwards usually brought her back in control, but it hardly worked this time. Walking down the corridor, she balled her fists to hide the emerging water.

"Ugh…" She winced, noticing a trail of waterdrops behind her.

The corners of Rize's mouth went down, trembling. Livid and anxious, she refused to accept that nothing of her doing would make her palms dry. She gritted her teeth.

"Four, three, two…"

The flash of a memory made her heart skip a beat. A confused pair of feline eyes looked up at her as if she was mental. The embarrassment flushed away her confidence, and with it the thin layer of the dust under her feet.

"Argh! Come on!" Rize fumed, standing in a freshly made puddle.

Her shoes chuffing and her feet wet, she stormed forward. A trip to the library seemed like a foolish idea now. The only thing she wanted was to shout curses into Angie's face.

"Love," Rize spat the word quietly. "If I knew that talking to Amethyst would open a geyser in my hand, I would've kept my mouth shut." She zealously wiped her palms, but the water kept coming. "Demon take you!"

She froze. How could she have missed that? This nonsense of the water cycle started after they had met the demon in the Nightmare Lands.

But why? What happened that day? Rize plunged into memories, desperate to recall anything that could help. *Is it the pact's consequences that Rel warned me about?*

Getting ready, Rize flexed her neck and shook her arms.

"Amethyst will kill me," she whispered and closed her eyes. "Fine. Think about Koryn. M-hm-hm…" she hummed, waiting to be dragged away by the Dolmen magic. "No? Then…Stones? Think about the magic ancient stones. Big stones. Bi-i-ig glowing stones."

A familiar tension crawled over Rize's muscles, pulling her into all directions at once. This time she accepted the power, ready to travel through the fabric of space.

"Come on…It's the Dolmen of Attraction, which means it—"

"—attracts," a familiar smoky voice murmured at her ear.

Rize flinched and slipped, turning round. She fell onto the wet ground, covered with slimy algae. Her bag opened with a loud thud, and library tomes landed in the dirt with a merry chomp. She grunted.

"You possess a primitive and rather limited thinking when it comes to minerals and their magic, mortal." The tall man narrowed his glossy black eyes, devoured by the demonic canker. Two golden suns painted his irises the moment he fixated his gaze on her.

"Very flattering, Koryn," Rize muttered, rubbing her elbow. "I hit my arm because of you."

The demon smirked. The body of a wiry middle-aged man served him as his vessel. Covered with rough grey skin, bluish in places, it exposed the ugliness of postmortem lividity. A wreath of thorny twigs crowned Koryn's forehead, messing up his fair hair. Like the last time Rize saw him, he used a skirt of rotten foliage from the waist to the ground due to his legless body. He hovered above the ground, the dry leaves of his attire rustling.

"I hear your thoughts, Rize Keer," he said. "You're here to tell stories and to end our deal…Which isn't a pact. Your custodians overreacted."

"Oh, really?" she said, her voice flat. "Isn't it what a demon would say to make me more docile for another pact?"

"Please." Koryn rolled his eyes. "These men hardly understand their own nature, let alone mine. Demon pacts always require a drop of demonic canker. You were never in danger."

Rize nodded, gathering her books back into her bag.

"What do I smell?" she changed the subject, her nose crinkled. "It's like someone died after eating a bunch of spoiled eggs."

"Behold the wetland of the wilds. I chose the most appealing side," Koryn said with a welcoming gesture. "Do you like it?"

"It's a marsh," she said. "Though I find it surprisingly alluring."

"Must be the spores," the demon waved her off. "It took you long enough to discover the way back here."

"Wanted to save more stories for you," Rize said.

"Liar!" he said irately. "I might forgive you for good entertainment. Mind that I love games and stories that I can brag about to ocean turtles," Koryn said.

"Did you know that love is not a vendoring of conveniences?" Rize looked up, recalling Angie's lecture. "One healer told me that."

"Funny," he smirked. "Is that what they teach you in the fancy barracks?"

"The Academy, yes." She sighed. "I guess that's not the breakthrough I had expected."

"Stubbornness and ingratitude," the demon grinned hungrily. "My favourite energies for a snack."

Rize cringed, imagining him scooping into her like ice cream. She shook her head and the vision disappeared.

"I just want to control this thing," she said, demonstrating the running waterdrops on her hand.

Curious, Koryn hovered closer. "Only the inner flow can do this," he said and reached out to Rize. He slowly dived into her wavy hair, placing both of his hands behind her ears. "I'm saving our time," he said, cupping most of her skull. "Stay still."

Rize gulped, feeling his deadly cold fingers on her skin. In a blink, she saw fragments of her memories rushing faster than the wind. The demon examined her mind, slowing the moments he considered worth watching. Those images hurt. She frowned but remained still, fighting the waves of pain.

"Was that enough stories for you?" Rize rubbed her throbbing temples when he finished.

"For now." Koryn gently pulled away and hovered back. "You finally took responsibility for your life choices and learned to ignore the pride that used to drag you down." He took a breath, though Rize doubted his dead body needed that much air to speak. "And you received the worst emotional dyad as a reward. Ironic! It will teach you that hard work is never worth it."

"Don't remind me," Rize moaned. "I knew the problem with the lightning. It emerged when I became angry or frightened. But this," she waved her hand and several drops joyfully scattered off her fingertips, "is messed up."

"One petty gemstone might help it, if you want." He pointed to the right.

Rize glanced, following his thumb.

"I was wondering where you placed it," she said and headed to the Dolmen.

Malachite veins, embedded into mossy stones, sparkled in the sun. They reflected pumping energy, glowing with a mysterious green light, which exposed carved delicate glyphs and circular letters.

"Hello there," Rize whispered. The veins gleamed in response a bit brighter.

"You seek wisdom to understand your path," Koryn said. "The stones will speak through me. Ask your questions."

"I know the rules." Rize crossed her arms. "You have no right to share its energy without the payment. What's your price?"

"Leave your satchel here," Koryn said. An eerie glisten touched his eyes as he smiled.

"But...I need it," Rize said doggedly.

The demon ignored her. Patient and calm, he reached his hand forward.

Her hands on her hips, Rize hesitated. The Dolmen began glowing brighter as if encouraging her to trust its guardian.

"Fine," she said and passed the bag, feeling foolish. "Can I ask my question now?"

"We are all ears." Koryn bowed his head, playing with her.

Her brow furrowed, Rize anxiously rubbed her chin.

"I want to understand how the water element impacts human nature," she said. "What do I need to master its force?"

The Dolmen flashed, and its vibrant lights spread across the wet ground. The energy resonated between the creaking trees and shallow puddles. Rize cowered, feeling its vibration in her stomach. When it all stopped, she looked at Koryn with anticipation.

"Long story short, stop fighting the current, dive in and see where it gets you," the demon said.

"Seriously?" Rize deadpanned. "Give me the details."

Koryn took a deep breath and cleared his throat, annoyed.

"If everyone follows the expected route while you resist it, doesn't it make you a rebel?" he said slyly. "The system will either break or kill you, Rize Keer. Would you like to be removed from it or become its vessel?"

Rize gritted her teeth and crossed her arms like a child.

"Can't I create a system of my own?" she said.

The demon paused and turned away lazily. Taking a deep breath, he closed his eyes and muttered. "Your pride is delicious."

Her heart shrinking, Rize stepped back. The demon licked his upper lip and put his blueish fingers over them. It took him a while to come back to his senses.

"The water," he murmured with a lustful smile on his face, "is a creator of life. *Your* creator. When you accept the world with its beautiful ugliness, you'll find your peace."

"Are you…" Rize frowned, finally figuring out what she had witnessed. "Are you drunk?"

"Didn't mean to offend you," Koryn drawled. The corners of his gravely pale lips went up. "Please, come back? You got your answer, after all."

"Right," she nodded. "Why is everyone saying different things, then?"

The demon caressed the Dolmen and its malachite veins glimmered. Getting brighter with each second, the stones greedily sucked out variegated matter from its guardian.

"There's no right response." His voice sober, Koryn finally gave her the answer. "The water takes the shape you provide it. For instance, give it a pipe, and you'll lose it both ways." He laughed. "One can't accept its energy unless one's vessel is complete. The same rules apply to the dyad that mortals call love."

The demon seemed tired and even more dead than he already had been.

"Why can't emotions be simple?" Rize sighed.

"They can. It's you who overcomplicates everything." Koryn shrugged. "But I like it. You feed me better than any other mortal creature. Your mood swings are so juicy and nurturing that even one meeting a month can saturate us both," he said, and leaned on the Dolmen.

The stones glowed again as if in agreement.

"Rel will be delighted to hear that," Rize grumbled, trying to wipe the last five minutes from her memory.

"A hooded boy with terrible hair?" the demon asked. A smirk full of disgust appeared on his face. "Stop hunting for his appreciation if you want your hands dry."

"I need his guidance. He never doubts or dithers. I wish I had that confidence," Rize said, getting bleak. "It's like he has a plan for everyone..."

"Mortals who are certain in their every move are the scariest creatures of all — predators. A leader's path is paved with decayed innocence. Imagine someone who sacrificed one's easy life for such an experience." Koryn tilted his head, a wicked grin on his face. "A little human. He's always armed. Always ready. As I see it, this Rel is made of self-hatred. He hides so much, trapped by his nature, when he should do the opposite. Choose your idols carefully."

Rize looked away, a crease on her forehead. She never thought about the price Rel had paid to become the man he was. Truth be told, she knew little of him and could hardly say if he was a good man. His lessons helped. His status saved her. He told her about his *sign* of greatness. For a short time, he was a friend she had never had. Rel trusted her.

Why? she thought.

"Excellent question!" Koryn praised her thinking.

"Do you know?" Rize asked as demanding notes pitched in her voice.

The Dolmen hummed, painting the wet ground with its eerie, green lights.

"It does," Koryn pointed to the side. "But we don't intervene in mortal lives for free." He crossed his arms, basking in the knowledge he refused to share.

"Not even by a bit?" Rize played along.

"The only thing I'll say is," he touched the Dolmen as if listening to its humming song, "something's changing. I can sense it in my demonic guts and smell it in the wind. The Universe's grip tightens, and shadows are waiting to break free."

"Maybe you ate something," Rize deadpanned. "Try to find a comfy bush."

"Shut it!" Koryn cut her off. "Look at the sky."

Rize lifted her gaze, frowning at the sunshine. Two luminaries moved towards each other slowly, but still visible.

"Huh," she said. "I forgot the eclipse is happening this week."

"The Radiance will change your Sun this month," the demon said, pleased by her answer. "Mortals always use celestial events for their dark deeds."

"I live near the Great One himself. Even two of them, as you've learnt from my memories. I'll be fine. Now, send me to the Academy, please." She knocked the Dolmen like it was a door. "I have a meeting to attend."

***

After changing her wet clothes, which smelled worse than a barrel of rotten eggs, Rize rushed to the pub. She impatiently made her way through the packed street whilst academicians and custodians enjoyed their time at shops and outside cafes.

Squeezing through the crowd, Rize stopped by a colourful banner. Promising all kinds of fun, it invited people to celebrate the upcoming eclipse and to welcome a new luminary on the pub terrace. She smirked seeing a lazy sketch of fancy pints and chicken wings.

"Must be Chour's idea," Rize muttered, and something heavy plastered her to the banner. "Ouch!"

"Sorry," a girl panted and continued walking, carrying a huge sack over her shoulder.

"Rookies…" Rize sighed, overlooking the crowd. She rarely chose this route due to its bustle and loud first years, but alas it was the shortest way to the town centre. She braced herself and stepped into the busy current.

Pacing in the river of people, Rize reached the place feeling tired and cranky. The pub doors opened with a subtle creak. A group of tipsy youngsters passed by, chanting a teasy verse. They were having a great time, but careless smiles on their faces made Rize roll her eyes. It felt like an eternity had passed when she could finally enter the building.

The kitchen and its chefs had problems. The distinct odour of burned food choked Rize by the entrance. She gasped, covering her nose and mouth, and walked a bit faster. Seeing Chour working at the bar, she headed to his counter. Still serving a customer, he pointed her in the right direction. Fashionably late, she finally found the Geckos.

Rize turned the corner and almost hit a tapestry screen that sectioned off four tables from the main hall. The whole squad, except Chour, had already drunk and eaten. Enjoying their privacy, they chatted loudly. Some were invested more than others.

His chair hit the floor as Bram jumped to his feet, telling the tale of his latest fights. He poked Crypt for attention. Distracted from his reading, the scientist winced at every loud noise, but said nothing. Angie and Laily ignored the men and chirped over the latest rumours, giggling like naughty children. Mars sat on the floor with Rose while Amethyst rested on the cat's sofa by the table. It looked like the three of them were discussing something without words.

Can the Worocks expand their telepathic web? Rize tilted her head.

"Nice booth you have here," she said instead, and looked around.

"Chour pulled some strings to make this cosy nook exclusively ours." Laily winked. "Speaking of sunshine…"

"Clear the way, Risotto!" Chour panted, carrying a dangerously craned tray. He reached the table and, holding his breath, served the drinks. "Holy elements, my back," he grunted, stroking his aching muscles after the last glass was placed. "I demand extra tips tonight!"

"You must pay me first," Sara said smugly. "Rize didn't come on time."

"After the shift, redhead." Chour waved her off and rushed away.

"What was that about?" Rize perched on an empty chair near Amethyst.

"Sorry, dearie," the pet drawled. "They refused to start the meeting without you, so I told them about your library obsession and—"

"—and we love easy money!" Sara raised her fist in victory. "Chour and I have our fun betting on some harmless things."

"I'd never suspected you were a gambler," Rize teased her.

"It's just the tip of the iceberg," Sara bragged. Her eyes sparkled with nasty little flames, and she added, "Check this out."

Sara pulled back her red hair. Curious, Rize watched as the strands slid away, exposing Sara's neck along with the side of her face that had always stayed hidden.

"Darkness, devour me..." Rize reached out to unevenly healed skin covered with horrible scars, but Sara twitched back. "What's happened to you?"

"I was a slave," she stated proudly, satisfied with the impression she made. "You've heard of slavery, right? Or is your land the place of endless festivals, and you never cared about the world's reality?"

"How nice. You sought out information on Lalu'Ed to impress the new girl," Crypt retorted, his nose buried in a book.

Surprised, Rize hid a smile. Crypt had never spoken in her presence before. His modulated voice was soothing and even calming at some points when she expected a nasal, grating sound instead. He possessed a confident and rather lecturing tone as if everyone around him were stupid.

"Although I doubt her civilisation is a fairy kingdom, intoxicated by prosperity. Following your logic, Chour should wear a fur coat, eat pickles for breakfast, and prance around astride an Itiz bear," he said and put the book away.

Tired, Crypt took off his glasses, then dropped them into his breast pocket. He avoided Sara's cold stare on purpose, as it seemed. His eyes wandered, fixating on objects that hung on the wall.

"Sara, your bias is based on hearsay," Mars joined them. "I've been to Ponktian, and it isn't that bad. Lalu'Edians are friendly and cheerful, but it hardly means everyone has rainbows instead of convolutions in their heads there."

"If not everyone, then most," Amethyst muttered.

Rize chuckled. "Rel's been to Lalu'Ed. You should trust his opinion more than ours."

"Oh?" Sara lifted her eyebrow and turned to their custodian. "Is that how you met?"

Unusually quiet, Rel finished his drink but made no reply. It looked like his thoughts were elsewhere, far away from the pub and his charges.

"Enough with the secrecy," Bram said, his voice raucous. "If I could choose a tale, I'd prefer listening to Rize than a slave girl."

"Hey!" Sara slapped his arm.

"Was that a mosquito bite?" Bram laughed.

Angie and Lally dropped their chat to witness the scene.

"What? You had a terrible life, then met me," Bram said and trapped Sara in a bear hug, standing behind her.

"I escaped and Academicians rescued me," Sara murmured, correcting him, and closed her eyes in pleasure.

A short pause lingered as everyone waited for Rel to say something. Finally, he straightened his hood and cleared his throat.

"Ready to become celebrities for a day?" Rel traded looks with Rize and Amethyst.

"I'll survive," the cat said as Rize zealously nodded multiple times.

"Alright." Rel hid a smirk. "You guys remember when I sent you away?" He looked over the Geckos to see if everyone was listening. "I had a solo mission while you were enjoying your freedom."

"Escorting the Great One, so I've been told," Chour said, bringing another tray with drinks. "This information cost me money, by the way."

"Let's not make it about you," Rel noted. "Although I praise your skills, this story is about them."

Rize elbowed Amethyst while the cat shifted his body, nervous under so many attentive eyes.

"So, imagine. Ponktian. It's the capital of the Lalu'Ed civilisation, by the way," Rel said. "The weather is a bit hot for my tastes, but nonetheless beautiful. It's the week of the Blossom Feast, after all."

"You spent it *there*?" Angie interrupted him, a note of resentment in her voice. "They say it's the best place for it in the world."

"Truly, everything that has leaves blooms there." Rel rolled his eyes. "Anyway, Eal and I arrived in Ponktian for business. No one from the ruling Council knew about the Great One's coming. They expected a man from the Citadel to pick recruits for the Academy, but—"

"They got a surprise," Laily sang and moved to let Chour sit by her.

"Indeed. I wasn't an exception," Rel said. "A mischievous mood hit our Great One, and he ran away from me. Literally!"

"I didn't know he did that on purpose," Rize said, and a short giggle left her chest. "Is that how he ended up at the Lowcity market?"

Rel nodded, his face grim. "I'm alone in a foreign city. Not only did I get lost, but also the Great One escaped my eyes in some strange-smelling market," he continued. "We'd been explicitly warned not to go there, but Eal was always drawn to shady stuff."

"Explains why he noticed Rize," Amethyst deadpanned.

"Suddenly, I saw a familiar goldish attire across the street," Rel continued. "I rushed at breakneck speed. What did I see? Soaked to the skin, the Great One was bragging before a woman who stood there, paralysed with anger, and saturating the ground with lightning without even noticing it." He finished his story, performing a believable pantomime.

Everyone laughed, appreciating the act.

"I hardly believe I crooked my face like that." Rize shook her head.

"Dearie, trust me, he's showing you in a favourable light," Amethyst said, causing another burst of laughter.

The loud cheer drowned out a subtle pop outside. It was sudden and barely audible, but Crypt left his glass half-finished and checked the outside view.

"What was that?" he asked, looking out the window.

"Probably the Chemical department's experimenting again," Rel said, waving his hand listlessly. "Come. Sit."

Crypt narrowed his eyes, staying where he was until Amethyst distracted him. The cat sniffed the air loudly, his nose up, and sneezed.

"Does anyone have a funny tickling in their noses?" The cat asked and shook his massive head, annoyed. "It burns my insides."

"The kitchen had an accident," Chour apologised.

"No, it's not that," the cat shook his head and sneezed again.

Rize noticed peculiar bumps on his back.

"Where did these come from?" she said, her hand on his fur.

Sara yelped.

"Stop!" she said and gestured Rize to move.

Reaching across the table, Sara gently shook Amethyst's fur. A bunch of tiny yellow petals fell to his paws.

"Well, hello there." Rize smiled. "Someone's been lying all day in a park."

"I haven't," the cat protested. "Chour brought some weird smelling weed to our flat and dropped it on me by accident."

"What?" Chour said, confused. "I've been working here since the morning."

Amethyst tilted his head, puzzled. "But I *saw* you. Talked to you! You came in and put them on Rize's desk!"

"What happened then?" Rel frowned.

"I…" Amethyst pricked his ears, thinking. "I yelled at him, and he took everything away. Left the place."

Another pop, much louder this time, rumbled outside. The pub visitors began murmuring. Some left their seats to see what caused the trouble. Dozens of worried voices poured out to the street.

"I was *here*," Chour insisted and came up to examine the cat's fur.

"Who came to the dorm then?" Amethyst barked. "Your twin?"

"Good question." Rize traded looks with her pet.

"Well?" Amethyst created a telepathic bond.

"Remember the warning from Mar'Anna? She said that there was a traitor in Rel's squad. What if one simply looks like us?" Rize thought. *"Her seer won't know the difference, right?"*

"A shapeshifter?" the cat frowned. *"We must tell them."*

"Not yet."

Rize squinted her eyes and tried to read the room. Everyone seemed genuinely worried.

"Wait. See that thing there?" Sara pointed. "To your left, Chour. No! Argh, let me do this."

She crawled over the table, empty glasses scattering with a loud clank. "Here, see?" she carefully pulled an inflorescence out of Amethyst's fur. "Is this the weed you were talking about?"

The cat nodded.

"Do you know what it is?" Sara said, showing Chour what she retrieved.

The young man opened his mouth but then shut it, raising his finger. He nervously pointed at an empty glass. Sara dropped the plant inside.

"Seeing your reaction, I assume it's poisonous," Sara smirked.

The Geckos jerked back out of instinct, making her laugh.

"What's funny?" Rize said, embarrassed.

"I'm resistant to many poisons." Sara shrugged, and a smug smile emerged on her face.

"Really?" Rize said.

"We ran some tests a long time ago to find the explanation," Crypt said, avoiding the eye contact. "Sara is one-eighth Lzon,"

"But you look…smooth," Rize mumbled.

"You think all half-breeds have scales?" Sara scoffed. "One-eighth is nothing. My hands are a bit webbed." She showed off her fingers proudly. "That's it."

"Very entertaining story, love." Chour grabbed the nasty glass. "Let me burn this plant safely."

Muttering curses to himself, the young man headed for the staff room. Meanwhile, Angie covered Amethyst's nose and whispered a healing spell.

"Do you know what it was, *nie*?" Angie asked the moment Chour came back.

"My people call this flower Hen Blindness. It's not supposed to grow here," he assured the Geckos. "Don't know what's going on, but I like it less with every second."

"Nothing ever happens with us inside the Academy grounds," Laily supported his mood. "What if—"

"Stop the panic," Bram cut her off. "How poisonous is that thing?"

All eyes were on Chour.

"It's a harmless buttercup that grows in fields," he recalled. "However, if you pick even one, the stem oil can irritate your eyes and cause short-term blindness."

"How many flowers were there?" Rel interlocked his fingers and leaned on a table.

"A bunch?" Amethyst looked to the side, trying to remember. "They barely fit the desk. The petals were all over the floor."

"Our dorm was clean when I came back," Rize said. "It doesn't make sense."

"Someone dared to attack us and tried to cover it up," Crypt distracted himself from observing the street and came back. "Any thoughts, Rel?"

"A shapeshifter, no doubt. Good logistics, but he's poorly informed."

"What's the point in targeting the newbies?" Sara said. "They are weaker than Chour and know nothing about any ops we handle."

"You'll boast later," Rel said and cupped his face, exhausted. "I need to think."

The third pop thundered nearby, making everyone flinch. Ringing and cracking, the window glass trembled in its frame but remained whole. Rize looked out from behind the screen. The pub got chaotic. Someone shrieked, paralysed by fear, while others ran outside in panic. Without saying a word, she passed through the main dining hall, and left the building. Amethyst followed her steps.

Chapter 14
FIGHTING THE CURRENT

The town centre became a disturbed hive. People ran away, screamed, bumped into each other, and fell, stunned by the sheer fear of what they had witnessed. Those who stayed home leaned out of their windows, trying to figure out what caused the chaos. Rize followed their gaze.

Crypt whistled as he joined Rize and Amethyst. "Holy elements…"

Puffs of smoke billowed far beyond the Citadel. Confused, academicians and recruits stared at the five towers, watching as one of them crumbled down. A short gasp ran across the crowd and a hot wave swallowed all who huddled in the street.

A gust of scorching wind caressed Rize's skin, soaking her hair in the acrid scent of smoke. She shivered. Her heart beat fast, sending cold heat down her spine.

A bonfire crackling.

Her lips pursed and Rize moaned, getting feverish. She erased the scent from her mind, yet it found her again. A vision of Ponktian, the city she grew up in, floated up from the pile of troubled memories. Her knees weak, she stepped back and almost fell but Crypt caught her, awkwardly stretching his arm to the side.

"Pardon me. I'm better at catching objects than people," he said and crossed his arms, which looked more like a self-soothing hug. "You okay?"

"W-what?" Rize said, losing focus.

The murmur of unrest brewed in the distance, but nobody moved from the street. Charmed by the unravelling calamity, people raised their hands one by one, then put them down, making a wave. Rize looked up. A shroud of gloomy, grey clouds covered the sky and painted the street with tin colours.

Another gust of wind washed Rize over with its stifling odour. She watched as dusty flakes gracefully floated in the air before them. Catching clots of fluffy, airy matter into their hair, people were blanketed with grey ash.

"Looks like a snowfall," Crypt said, rubbing a lump of greyness in his fingers.

"I assure you it's not snow." Rize trembled, brushing the flakes off of her clothes.

"You'll be the first who understands," Amethyst thought into Rize's head. *"These were Mar'Anna's words."*

Suddenly the crowd moved. Academicians scattered away, twisting their faces in dread. People bumped into each other, screamed, but kept running.

"We need to warn the others," Rize said and dragged Crypt back to the pub, leaving him no chance to protest.

Rize ran. The blood boiled in her veins, making it impossible to think. A black shadow crawled over her eyes, plunging her into animalistic fear. As if trapped in a dark tunnel, she could barely see her way.

Chour noticed her first. "Hey, what's wrong?"

"We must go." Rize ignored him and grabbed Rel by his arm. "Now!" She tugged him harder.

Rel pulled off a clump of dusty ash from her hair. He tensed, clearly recognising the substance, but said nothing. His jaw clenched as he looked at Rize unblinking, which made his charges nervous.

"Everyone, go back to your dorms and prepare. Rize, Amethyst, and I will go to the arsenal. Let's meet in fifteen minutes...You know where." He jerked his chin, ordering Rize and Amethyst to follow him outside.

Academy Town simmered in fear. It spread across the streets as a contagious disease, plaguing people's minds.

Rel, Rize, and Amethyst joined the hectic crowd. Their eyes darted. The trio moved fast but the current fought their pace. Dodging panicking recruits, Rize split from the group. Rize tried to keep up, but Rel evaded obstacles with a dancer's grace while she bumped into everyone on her way. Seeing this, Amethyst lowered his head and roared at those who had lost their heads in panic.

"Do we need something in particular from the arsenal?" Rize asked when they entered the arena grounds. "I doubt we need weapons at all."

"I don't," Rel said. "We came to seal the arsenal. If this attack was made by the same people who ruined your city, they are poor mages. I won't let them use our weapons against us. Especially firearms."

"I already have five questions." Rize held the door that led to the arsenal, waiting.

"Later," Rel snorted and tossed her daggers, Chour's axe and Sara's knives as one bundle.

The weapons untied in the air, making it impossible to catch. Rize gasped. Hands up, she bent her fingers in an easy-done gesture, making the blades float.

"It wasn't a test. Sorry. I didn't check the belts on them," Rel said, pinching his nose. "I'm a bit distracted today." He went silent, getting ready to conjure.

"No worries," she said, collecting the weapons hanging in the air.

A thin shadow slid back and forth in the corner of her eye. She looked down. Amethyst's tail was sweeping the floor while his feline body tensed, each hair standing on end.

"What's wrong?" she thought into Amethyst's head.

"Don't you feel it?" the pet glanced up. His nose quivered, whiskers flickering.

Rize's talisman jiggled under her shirt. The gem became hot, absorbing magic that came from the outside. She pulled the chain out and frowned. She had seen Rel using his power many times, and its source never troubled Amethyst.

His arms spread, Rel bent his fingers as if he tried to find hinges in the veil of their reality. He sighed with relief the moment he sensed what he'd been looking for.

"Close his ears," Rel commanded. "This spell has undesirable side effects for animals."

"Like what?" Rize followed the order.

"Like bursting eardrums." He clapped once, raising a vibrant, ringing storm.

The fabric of space shook under his hands, ripping objects that seemed real. Rize squinted, watching shapes blur until the room, with all its contents, vanished.

"That's it," Rel said, hands on his hips. The arsenal became a poorly cleaned cupboard.

"Is it what I think it is?" Rize lamented as her eyes widened.

"It's nothing," Rel waved her off. "You should see Laily at work one day. I'm nothing compared to her. The Monokiese Phantasm school is much better than our Department of the Illusion Arts here."

"Can I…Can you…Why didn't you…" Rize stuttered, confused.

"She wants to learn how to do it," Amethyst translated her mumblings.

"I'll talk to the Head of Air School when the next semester starts," Rel said, closing the door. "Let's go now."

The town was drowning in dusty ashes. Rel chose a winding route through small, unlit streets adjacent to the narrow alleys, hidden from innocent bystanders. Rize and Amethyst used these passages often during their first weeks.

"These flakes make my fur itchy. Where are we going, by the way?" Amethyst asked, shaking off annoying ashes again and again.

"To my place," Rel said, coming up to the end of the street. He gestured to take cover behind him. "We always meet in my basement when the emergency happens."

"I thought you lived in the Citadel like the Great One," Rize whispered.

Rel peeked out from behind the corner. He carefully observed the setting. Panicking people stopped them from crossing the road unnoticed. The hooded man lurked back.

"On paper, I don't. In reality? I do. The Elders prefer to keep an eye on me even when I sleep. My very existence is dangerous for the system, remember? However, according to the law, the Great One and his advisor must live separately without any possibility to discuss matters outside working hours," Rel explained. "My title and all that comes with it is a fiction. Everyone from infants to rulers are supposed to believe the made-up legend."

"So, the Empress of Tsaan doesn't know about your…" Amethyst paused to choose a better word, "…uniqueness? Yeah, right."

"I said, 'supposed to'." Rel chuckled. "I never said they do."

Finally, the recruits on the road remembered that they were trained fighters and charged away like a well-organised squad. When the street became deserted, Rel left their little hideout and beckoned Rize and Amethyst to follow him.

They swiftly crossed the road, slipped into the opposite alley, and kept moving forward. Paved with a large mountain stone, the alley went down an incline that led to a dead-end.

"Isn't this your house? The plate says it belongs to the advisor," Rize pointed behind her shoulder, passing the front gate.

"We'll enter the basement directly," Rel said, slowing down his walk. "A couple of cleverly made spells, and I always remain incognito. No one knows this way in."

"I suppose for your lifestyle, it's necessary," she grumbled.

"Speaking of sneaking and secrets." Amethyst glanced around, checking if they were still alone. "How many Geckos know the truth about you?"

"Angie and Laily," Rel said. "Which means everyone."

"Are you sure this is the right way?" Rize looked at the tall walls around them, confused.

"Silly question. Of course, I'm sure," Rel said, and stopped to run his hand over the stone facade. "Demon...I can never find it from the first try."

Rize and Amethyst traded looks.

"Well, we'll wait till you've caressed all the stones," the cat scoffed.

"Right," Rize supported his joke. "Nothing serious happened. Ash? Who cares? It doesn't look like the Blossom Feast case at all."

"Blossom Feast, now this...It seems to me we should never party together, Risotto." Rel said, leaning his ear to the wall. "It always ends with a local catastrophe."

"Maybe you'll finally tell us what you're looking for?" Rize lost her patience and leaned against the wall, annoyed.

A gasp of surprise left her chest as she fell through. Amethyst hissed, seeing his human disappear into the solid wall. The savoury curse announced Rize was alive, though in pain.

"Oh, you found the way in," Rel drawled mockingly. "Good girl."

The hooded man and the cat stepped into the illusion and disappeared.

***

Rize bumped into smelly, old clothes resting on hangers. She pushed them gently, squinting out of a loud creak over the rail, and stepped forward. Landing on the tile floor, she emerged from a tall cabinet that was cleverly disguised as a wardrobe.

"It's so…Rel-ish," she said, letting Amethyst out. The cat snorted.

Ignoring her remark, Rel turned the lights on. Although the basement had a low ceiling with a sneaky hatch in the middle, it looked spacious and clean. Numerous shelves held old tomes, maps, smoked food, water flasks, and dried herbs.

A couple of racks with exquisitely crafted outfits rested by the secret passage they had come from. Charmed, Rize stroked the delicate weaving.

"Is it for healers?" she asked, studying the armour.

"Yes. Angie admires our local tailor," Rel said, arms crossed. "He blabbers too much, if you ask me, but knows the craft. He makes casual clothes too if you're interested."

"Maybe…" Rize stepped back.

"Why do you always overcomplicate things, Rel?" Amethyst grumbled, losing his temper after the hard day. "Why can't you use

144

a normal door? What is it this time? Spies? Assassins from the Dark Hundred? Your mother?"

Rel laughed hysterically, his head back. He rubbed his face as if helping himself to shake off the stress.

"Your mistress taught history, right?" he said, annoyed by Amethyst's questions. "There can't be two Great Ones. It hurts any political regime in all civilisations. You know what happened last time. One died under mysterious circumstances, the other went insane. I'm against any of these scenarios. I just want to make sure I stay alive, though the Elders have their own plans."

"Meaning?" Amethyst pricked his ears.

"Oh, you'll be shocked finding out how many times they tried to get rid of me."

"By 'get rid of' you convey…" Rize half-arched her eyebrow.

"Tarnish, eliminate, murder, kill, poison," Rel said. "Not necessarily in this particular order but…Surely you get the gist. When I was in my third year at the Academy, they almost killed me in my own bed," he shared, his voice bitter. "Eal refused to even consider that case. 'You had it coming! You shouldn't be friends with the emperor's daughter! The Tsaanish are jealous racists!'," Rel mimicked the Great One.

"I'm confused," Rize stopped his performance. "The Elders just observe the Great One's decisions. They have no real power. How could they arrange that and avoid the punishment?"

"They are cunning mages. It doesn't make them useless. You've seen Elder Air in Lalu'Ed. He's quite efficient, don't you think?" Rel said. "One of a few allies I still have in the Citadel."

"Wait a second," Amethyst ignored his sentiments. "What are you telling us? The Great One doesn't control civilisations now? The Elders do?!"

Rel nodded, his face grim.

"But—" Rize stuttered.

"So, what? He dances around the old bipedals and you hide. Really?!" Amethyst snapped. "Together you could've smashed them like bugs!"

"A bunch of organised elderly mages can overthrow anybody by a simple assassination," Rel said. "I bleed like mere mortals, and they have money and agents all over the world."

"Fun," the cat deadpanned.

"Listen, Eal is smarter than me at these under-carpet games. He *actually* helps civilisations by tickling the Elders' schemes," Rel said. "He knows when to smile, to act stupid, to turn the blind eye. That's why they enjoy his reign and are afraid of me going rogue. I'm…sickeningly unpredictable."

"What did you do to make them angry?" Rize frowned.

Rel rubbed his neck, stalling.

"It was the year when Lalu'Ed had a financial crisis because of the currency drop. It was planned and played out well to some of the Elders. You see, it was their *turn* to stuff their pockets and blame the poor," Rel said. "I got excited and might've threatened to expose their shady scheme to the public. The plan was childish, so was the state of my mind, but some Elders are extremely touchy subjects. They rarely forget things. So, their revenge was spectacular."

"Oh?" Rize said stiffly.

Waiting for the rest of the story, she and Amethyst made themselves comfortable.

"It happened much later, which certainly dulled my vigilance," Rel said. "The Elders agreed to make me a custodian with immense reluctance. They couldn't deny my request, mainly because of Eal — the Great One's wish is still the law to them. Although Eal paid little attention to my everyday life, he always took my side. He

trusted me. It was his idea to make me an advisor. It solved two problems at once. The Elders and their little servants could keep an eye on me, and I would sleep peacefully, secured by the Great One's guards."

Rel sighed, haunted by his past, and leaned against the wall.

"When the Geckos legally became elite fighters," he said, "my squad received the first recon operation. At that time, the squad included only Laily, Angie and..." he paused, "...and Hope."

Rize and Amethyst traded worried looks.

"Sounds like a group, not a squad," Amethyst joked to end the awkward silence.

Rel ignored his words. "The girls were thrilled. They'd dreamt of serving the Great One for ages. And I...Well, I was glad to escape Academy Town unaccompanied."

"What was your job?" Rize tilted her head, curious.

"Investigate the suspected human trafficking," Rel said. "We kept one tribe under surveillance."

"Wow." Rize gulped.

"Slave traders crossed the Yenemi border which was and still is a violation of the Citadel law," Rel continued. "So, we had to watch their movements, locate the marketplace if there was one, and then report on the results. Reinforcements would've helped us rescue the kidnapped people, but that op turned out like nothing we were promised."

"What went sideways?" Amethyst said, coming closer.

"Everything," Rel's voice cracked as if someone grabbed his throat. He took a moment to recover. "The reinforcements never came. We lost Hope, and I...I had to evolve with the events to save the rest of us. I used more magic than a common academic could."

"Angie and Laily learned about your greatness," Amethyst guessed.

"Yeah," Rel uttered. "No one can supply the emotional flow for spellcasting longer than a couple of minutes."

"No one normal, you mean?" Rize's lips quivered in a sad smile.

"Magic never has enough of you," Rel said. "It consumes the flow fast and drains people to madness or death. That's why self-control is *so* important. Honestly, it's better to kick someone with a stick than supply magic with unstable emotions."

Speaking up seemed wrong after what Rel had told them. Rize waited patiently, feeling sorry for him. A few people could've survived what he experienced in one lifetime.

Amethyst paced forward and poked the hooded man.

"What?" Rel muttered.

"I crave details, bipedal. Your story has black spots. As usual," the cat said and wagged his tail, annoyed.

"Amethyst," Rize hissed.

"That's fine. Really. You need to know everything," Rel said and took a deep breath. "We went through the portal, and I knew straight away we were in trouble. Swamps, ugly bushes, all the beauty of the Nightmare Lands welcomed us that day. The only thing that stood out was a frightened ginger girl, baring a sharpened stick. 'Stay away!', she said. She desperately tried to appear dangerous." Rel smirked at his boots.

"It was you who helped Sara," Rize had a wild guess. "She said the academicians rescued her after she escaped."

"She never talks openly about it," Rel shook his head. "Some may think that she got a place by my side out of pity...or worse. Seriously though, her will to bury the past is enviable. Sara learned quickly and trained a lot. Just like you two." He paused, thinking. "I'm sorry somebody assaulted you at your home, Amethyst. It's my fault. You are under my command, so…” he failed to finish his thought and went quiet.

“You, Sara. What happened next?” Amethyst reminded him the real subject of their conversation.

“As we had landed on alien territory, Sara helped us out. She saw that we posed no threat, so she told us about herself and where she came from,” Rel said. “I invited her to join us and to ‘help in the name of the Great One and our Universe!’ Ha-ha.”

“Pompous,” Amethyst grunted.

“We were young and stupid. Sara had never seen the weapons, armour, and magic that we possessed,” Rel agreed. “Idiots met to find their adventures.”

“Did she really come with you?” Rize asked. “Right after she escaped?”

“No. She was too scared,” Rel said. “I used one of our portal seeds, and she left the Nightmare Lands for good. Thanks to Sara, we learned that the settlement from which she had fled *was* the marketplace itself. Moreover, slaves were sold by top Academy officials, and the Elders knew about it.”

“Who would’ve doubted that?” Amethyst spit his sarcasm. “Once you had a look, everything became clear. Just like the attack in Lalu’Ed, right? Do you still think that the Council and the Great One rigged it? Wait, was it the underwater Lzons? No! Elder Air? Hm. Maybe they did it together. I really can’t keep up with all your theories.”

Rel slowly tilted his head as if controlling every fibre in his muscles. He granted Amethyst a baleful stare.

“One glance was enough for me, *pet*, because I recognised the people involved in the deal. I lost a person there, for Universe’s sake!” Rel fumed. “As for Ponktian, Eal indeed had a personal touch in what had happened. My mistake was to suspect him of crime when he tried to save the day. I know the reason for his trip to Lalu'Ed because he told me about it recently. I chose to believe him."

"Please, stop fighting," Rize said, tired. "The ash is freaking me out. What's our plan?"

Amethyst and Rel exchanged irritated looks.

"Firstly, I'm going to discuss the plan of action with people I trust," Rel said. "Secondly, we'll head to the Citadel, where I'm supposed to be now."

"Speaking of trust," Rize muttered. "I must tell you something."

"Risotto? You of all people?" Rel teased her, seeing her guilty doe-eyed look.

"Remember when you took a day off?" she asked and started pacing the floor. "The empress summoned me."

Amethyst crinkled his muzzle. "I'd say she kidnapped you but, please, go on."

"The soothsayer took me to Mar'Anna—"

Rel rubbed his forehead and sighed heavily, taking off his hood.

This sudden act of trust silenced Rize. Afraid to breathe, she stared at his profile, framed by the dim basement lights. Rel had prominent brow ridges, which granted him the never-ending tired look she had seen so often. His pointy nose had a bumpy bridge as if it had been broken many times. His long dark hair scattered messily, caressing his jawline and weather-bitten cheeks.

Rize blinked, hoping he wouldn't turn into the same mysterious Rel she knew. There was something wild and troubled in his look. As if annoyed, he pulled his hair back, exposing the *sign* of greatness on his forehead.

"Well?" Rel said, turning to her. His fringe slowly fell back, covering the sign. "Why did she summon you?"

Speechless, Rize stood baffled until Amethyst butted her thigh.

"Sorry. She said that there was a traitor among your men," Rize babbled. "And that only I would understand that something was wrong, and that I must act…or be active? Can't remember it now, really."

"Mar'Anna informed me about the traitor. She wanted to protect me," Rel said. "What about the soothsayer? Was she with you at the time?"

"Y-yes. The empress said that she had a vision of me doing everything right," Rize stammered. "But I don't even know what! That talk was delirious. She believed that if I left the Academy, you would die, Rel."

"A heavy burden," Amethyst said. "Should we be worried?"

Rize looked at her custodian. He seemed flattered, though his boots received a sad smirk instead of a grin.

"The future depends on ourselves: our actions and their consequences, of which there are a great many," Rel said. "No one should dance around vague prophecies and visions."

"Said the Dreamcatcher," Amethyst grunted.

"What I do happens naturally. I don't resist it," Rel explained patiently. "I obey the force that is a part of me. There was no ritual. No sacrifice. I didn't *make* myself see things, unlike the empress's seers."

"You stopped fighting the current," Rize said, and their eyes met.

"I'm still trying," Rel muttered, getting grim again.

A sudden thud rang out over their heads. Rel frowned as they heard the footsteps upstairs.

Chapter 15
IF I DIE YOUNG

"It took them longer than I thought," Rel muttered.

His fingers nervously drummed over the wall. He looked at Rize clearly thinking if continuing his story was worth it. He came up to Rize and, to her greatest shock, gently stroked her hair.

"Listen," Rel said, his hand on her shoulder. "Once, you followed a prediction from the very same seer, and only she knew where it would lead you in life. But *we* are the masters of our destiny, Rize. If the Lady in White remained silent, you'd have rejected the demon's offer. I'm sure of that. Don't you hate the idea of someone controlling your path?" His eyes darted. "Or using you for their plan?"

"I…" Rize pursed her lips, ashamed. "I guess I'm used to someone supervising my actions and punishing me when I become daring."

Rel nodded.

"You are not in Lalu'Ed anymore," he said, a grim look on his face. "Use your own head."

Amethyst flinched as someone stomped above their heads, but Rel remained calm. The only thing that broke his tranquil posture was his uneven breath. Looking down at Rize, he hypnotised her with the confidence that instilled safety and peace.

Her hands grew wet, though it had nothing in common with the magic surges Rize had faced before. A strange tingling swirled in her stomach as her heart skipped a beat. Charmed like prey before a predator, she watched him moving his lips, saying words of wisdom, and smirking. It made no sense that her heart squeezed in a pang of pain. She wanted to shake off his hand but couldn't, feeling nothing but utter awe.

"If I die young, so be it," Rel said. His voice didn't tremble, as if that thought had been his companion for years. "I'll be happy because *my* conscious choices will beckon death to me. I chose fair fighters who would be with me when it happens." He looked up, hearing more footsteps and swiftly pinched Rize's chin, playing with her. "As for the traitor among us, I'll deal with him when the time is right."

"So, you know who it is?" Amethyst said, his eyes widening.

Giving nothing but a cheeky smirk in response, Rel began humming a merry tune. A hatch opened in the ceiling with a creak. Angie jumped down. Minding her head, she stooped as her head touched the ceiling.

"Hey, help us down, big woman," Bram hurried her.

Angie hesitated. She watched Rel hastily putting on his hood and traded a surprised look with Rize. Finally, she glanced back at her custodian, her eyebrow arched.

"They're here," the healer whispered over her shoulder.

One by one, the Geckos joined them in the basement. Rize noticed all of them donned leather or fabric armour adorned with belts, pouches, and metal plates. Even Rose had a peculiar piece of gear to show off.

"Catch, Risotto!" Mars tossed her a huge linen bag. "For Amethyst. I bought it for Rose, but she never grew up to this size."

Her hand up, Rize almost missed the bag. Turning it around, she found a knot and tugged it gently, revealing what was inside.

"It's armour," she breathed out, pulling out a piece of laced tanned leather.

Dread enveloped Rize for the first time this day. She looked down at Rose. The Worock's vest perfectly matched her feline frame. Its darkened metal inserts framed her ribcage like the bones of an unknown creature.

"No room for jokes from now on, Meatball," Bram granted Amethyst a mocking look. "We brought something for your mistress as well. Try it on."

Sara handed Rize a partly torn duffel bag and took her place behind Bram, hands on his shoulders. Caressing his neck, she squinted while a shadow of disgust lingered on her face. Seeing Rize's questioning stare, Sara smirked.

"Get dressed," she said and faked a smile.

Stepping back, Rize dropped both bags. Her hands trembling, she tried on a leather jacket. She buttoned up her new outfit and looked at a stained mirror nearby. The jacket was soft and made no sound while she moved, sitting like her second skin. The cuffs and buttons glistened eerily in the dim light but didn't attract unnecessary attention.

"Itizian leather," Crypt said, coming up closer. "It's a piece of a fine armour, despite the old-fashioned look. How does it feel?" he asked, and his gaze shifted to the nearest wall when Rize looked at him.

"Scary," she confessed and stroked her belly, getting used to the thick leather over it.

"The only thing that matters is you being able to fight and cast spells whilst wearing it," Crypt said light-heartedly.

"Is everyone here?" Rel looked around. "Where's Laily?"

"Closing the doors using all locks and spells," Chour grumbled, methodically stuffing herbs from the shelf into his pouches and pockets.

Rel and Angie locked eyes. Rize saw the healer give him a nod and his eyes darkened.

"I'm here. I'm here." Laily rushed into the basement, blabbering, and closed the hatch behind her. "Rel, honestly, we have little time."

"How many men?" he asked.

"I spotted two, but my spell detected the presence of many more," the blonde said, troubled. "No less than six. If we don't move soon—"

"I got it," Rel cut her off.

"What's wrong?" Bram murmured in pleasure while Sara massaged his neck. "Apart from the fact that you and Risotto ran away into the sunset like two girlfriends, clearly knowing something. Is this why your mansion surrounded?"

"You tell me. Why is it so?" Rel asked. An awkward pause lingered in the air. "Maybe you know something about it."

Rize looked around cautiously, hoping to meet a pair of confused eyes, but the Geckos remained focused. Only Amethyst and Rose stared at each other as if sharing their thoughts secretly.

"What's going on?" Rize thought, addressing Amethyst.

"It's not Bram," the cat replied.

"WHAT?!" Rize's eyes popped out.

"Act normal and don't distract me."

Amethyst cut off the contact, leaving Rize to deal with her confusion alone.

"I'm waiting." Rel tilted his head. "Speak."

"Why should I know something?" Bram smirked, surprised. "Ouch! Woman, don't push so hard! You will break my neck," he looked back and got a rich jab in his jaw.

Sara squeezed Bram with a neck-smashing grip, making him gasp for air. He tried to break free, but Mars punched him in the gut.

Thud.

Moan.

Cough.

Blood on the floor.

Bram jumped to his feet. His raging cry made the place rumble when he knocked over those around him like they were weightless toys. He pushed back, sending Sara and Mars into the air.

A gasp of pain. Mars fell, hitting his head. Sara crashed into the wobbly old crates by the wall. They broke, cracking under her body. She spat curses but rushed back to Bram again.

The situation unravelled so fast that Rize felt she missed half of it when she blinked. She stepped aside, tripped, and slumped to the floor. Someone's strong arms wrapped around her chest.

"Let them be," Angie panted and pulled Rize back to safety.

Amethyst lunged forward with a roar and knocked Bram down, letting Rose dig her fangs into the man. Shouts full of rage turned into silence. It lingered for a while, disturbed only by heavy breathing and growling cats.

Chapter 16
SHAPESHIFTER

"Could you stop just for a second?!" Rize said.

Ever since the real Bram had rushed from the basement side passage, he began painting his double's face with colourful bruises. Each time his fist hit the target, Rize winced, and her shoulders twitched.

"I." Bram hit a ringing slap. "Missed." A jab. "The whole." Another slap. "Day!"

"Stop!" Rize yelled, trying to grab Bram's arm that was three times wider than hers. "There's no need for this!"

"We are not a gardening community!" Rel lost his patience and pushed her away from the shapeshifter. "Let Bram do his work. We have no time for your drama."

"That's not a job!" Rize protested. "It's a slaughter."

"Rel…" Angie tried to calm her leader, but he ignored her.

He watched as Rize began pacing the floor, occasionally slowing down near Amethyst just to grant him a judgmental look.

"I can't believe you want to be a part of this," she said, lecturing her pet. "My people respect and value life. We are peaceful creatures, and bloodthirst is alien to our philosophy."

"To *Lalu'Edian* philosophy, dearie," Amethyst cut her off. "We are not there anymore. Evolve."

That was new. Her cat had never left her side when it came to a fight.

"That's insane." Rize shook her head.

"What did you expect?" Rel spat the words angrily. "That you'd move from Lalu'Ed, and I'd train you to join the department you like? Without any payment?!"

Rize stopped and stared at him in disbelief.

"You are *mine* until you decide to leave," Rel said. "What is it you want to master? Chemistry, physics, engineering? Maybe you have healing skills that I don't know of? Ah, wait." He snapped his fingers. "Illusion! It just slipped my memory."

Defeated, Rize couldn't handle his irate look and turned away.

"I promised you that I'd find you a spot if you want to study. I'm a fair custodian," Rel said. "If you feel the urge to restore justice, then try to find a commune like Angie and Laily did. Find a job like Chour! Do something peaceful. Do penance for evil deeds by helping society. I don't care!" He threw up his hands. "But now, you'll obey my orders, Rize Keer."

"So, we will keep him here? Torture? You think I don't understand where this is going?!" Rize lost her temper and a splash of water hit the floor. She groaned in disgust and swiftly wiped her hand. "I'm not killing people," she muttered.

Rel sighed heavily, pinching his nose.

"No one is going to kill the shapeshifter, Little Flower," Angie said softly.

"We just need to find out who sent him," Sara cooed, sharpening her knife. "Nothing more."

"Without any blood? Why have I come here then?" Bram was offended, kicking the unconscious double. "This worm knocked me down and took my place, y'all. I want to pay my respects!"

He wanted to kick the shapeshifter again but stopped hearing as his custodian cleared his throat.

"Bram!" Rel fumed. "How do you know about the secret passage to my basement?"

"But…M-m-m..." he gulped. "Everyone knows."

"Angi-i-ie?" Rel glared at her.

"Let us all calm down for a moment," Angie almost sang the words. Her hands up, she got ready for Rel flying off the handle.

"I'm. More. Than. Calm," he growled, proving the opposite. "Explain yourself."

"Everyone in this room knows about the passage, except for this worm, maybe." Bram kicked his double again. "As well as the fact that ya're not really an advisor, boss."

Rel stared at Bram like a trapped beast and missed when Laily came up closer.

"Well? Will you show us your *sign*, or I must take off your hood by force?" Laily said, and gently pulled the fabric.

"Only I can take it off, princess." Rel cracked under her childish request and smiled. "And now is not the time." He pursed his lips, then asked quietly, "When did you find out?"

"Does it matter?" Bram shrugged. "We're still here, following your orders."

"I should say, it's a bit insulting that you simply revealed yourself to Rize and Amethyst today." Angie pursed her lips. "This kind of knowledge must be earned."

"They earned it the day I met them," Rel said, enjoying her astonishment. "The day their city drowned in the very same ash we saw here today."

"You lost a bet again." Sara grinned, elbowing Chour. "Must be my lucky day."

"Do you really think I took money with me?" Annoyed, Chour showered her palm with imaginary coins.

"Enough chatting. Let's ask our new friend a couple of questions," Rel said, and crossed arms. "Tie the man. We'll take him with us to the Citadel."

"To what's left of it," Chour muttered and took ropes from a shelf.

Rize watched him making knots she had never seen before. She tilted her head, trying to understand the process.

"Cool, huh?" Chour bragged.

"It's impressive you remember what follows what," Rize said, looking at how the ropes intertwined.

"My father taught me, 'Each person is made of little things that build the character.' By my foolishness, I thought 'little things' were goods from a corner shop like needles, nails, and ropes. I couldn't fathom why people were made of mundane objects, and why I should count them as my companions…but I learned to use them."

"I'm shocked you haven't met your soulmate," Sara deadpanned.

"Ta-da!" Chour triumphantly demonstrated the ropes twisted around the shapeshifter. "He's all yours now."

"Great. I wanna have a word with him." Bram squatted before the shapeshifter and patted his cheeks. "Wakey-wakey, ugly face."

"Said my reflection," the shapeshifter croaked and winced, getting a slap.

"It can joke! Nice. I'm a comedian myself," Bram said happily, though his eyes mirrored nothing good. He grabbed the man's chin and craned closer. "Ya open your mouth to reply. If your answer is wrong, I'll make ya bleed. Good?"

Calm, as if interrogations were his usual ritual, the false-Bram nodded.

"Nodding is even better. Let's check if you're really that smart. Do ya see this little kitten?" Bram asked, turning the double's head so that he could see Amethyst.

A nod.

"Did ya bring poisonous herbs into his mistress's room?" Bram titled his head, his voice soft.

Another nod.

"Good. Now you'll tell my boss why ya did it." Bram stood up and crossed his arms, waiting.

"Naturally, to take her place," the false-Bram said, glancing at Rize. "Although I failed, I have plenty of intel on this squad. What a company…A half-breed, an abomination, a genius, a runaway princess, a bunch of orphans, and a useless toddler, along with two kittens. Impersonating Rize was the easiest way to get your leader's head."

Rel squinted his eyes. "Perfect. You like talking."

"He's also a decent mage," Bram said, rubbing his neck. "He knocked me out with one single spell."

"Why couldn't our Worocks spot him?" Sara said. "All humans have a unique scent."

"Especially Bram." Laily widened her eyes.

"He doesn't smell like a human," Rose said, her ears flattened. "I missed it. My bad."

"Amethyst fixed your mistake," Rel muttered. "I guess you're happy to finally have a backup."

Amethyst purred, his nose up.

"You are making progress in creating broad telepathic webs," Mars praised Amethyst. "Rose could connect six people only after two years of training with Grant."

"Stop exchanging pleasantries and get down to business," Bram barked. "Can ya identify the smell?"

"Mown grass," Amethyst said, sniffing the man. "Bipedals usually reek of sweat or aromatic oils, but not a lawn."

"Ideas?" Rel arched his eyebrow.

Chour shrugged. "It could be any decoction, even a medicinal one."

"Are you working for Stingray?" Rel said.

"You know the answer," the false-Bram mocked.

"Ya forgot the rules, mate." Bram grabbed the man's finger and broke it without even blinking.

Rize and the shapeshifter screamed. One out of terror, the other from pain. Angie facepalmed, mumbling something about the excessive violence, while the other Geckos supported Bram. As for Crypt, he continued tapping his screen as if nothing had happened.

"Demon take you." Sara spat on the floor. "Who sent you?!"

"Air fairies," the false-Bram tittered, fearless about another broken bone.

"Wrong answer!" Bram rejoiced and grabbed the man's middle finger. "One more chance. Who sent ya?"

"Your *true* ruler," the shapeshifter said, his eyes darkened.

"The Great One?" Laily said, lifting her eyebrow.

"I refuse to believe Eal is to blame. Many tried to put this thought into my head," Rel said. "No matter what, he'll always be on my side."

"Yeah, he cracked too fast." Sara pursed her lips, thinking. "Crack his other finger."

The front door upstairs smashed above their heads, making Rize flinch. The basement ceiling rumbled, letting out small clouds of dust.

"We need to go," Rel hurried his charges. "Chour, Angie. Do your thing, and let's move."

"Shall we do it by a spell or the old-fashioned way, colleague?" Angie asked mindfully.

"Allow me. I've cooked something special." Chour grabbed a piece of cloth and generously poured some odorous liquid over it. "Deep breaths, mate."

"What?" The shapeshifter winced in panic. "What is it?"

Covering the shapeshifter's nose and mouth, Chour held the cloth tight. A subtle mooing came out from the false-Bram as he tried to wiggle out. His legs jerking and hitting the floor, he zealously fought the grip that trapped him. Soon enough his body turned limp, and the man began drooling.

"He's asleep," Chour said, seeing Rize's troubled eyes.

"Finally. Clear the way!" Bram put the shapeshifter on his shoulder, and the Geckos left through the secret passage.

Chapter 17
FINGER-POINTING

Academy Town looked painfully empty and abandoned while the streets slept, resting in the embrace of the ash winter. Walking along the silent alley, Rize noticed people pushing back the curtains. They peeped out of their windows to see who marched to the Citadel then backed away, satisfied with the answer.

"What was in that tower?" Rize asked, looking at the collapsed building. "I don't remember."

"Archives," Rel muttered.

Angie's eyes became misty and red, though it was hard to tell why. The closer they were to the Citadel, the filthier the air became. They coughed, gasping, but continued moving.

"Wide open doors. No guards," Sara said quietly as they reached the Citadel.

"That's a bad sign," Bram agreed and shifted the limp body on his shoulder. "What's our plan?"

"Stay alert," Rel said, and entered the building first.

The Geckos carefully crossed a spacious hall and went upstairs, covering each other's backs. No living soul greeted them. There lay only corpses.

"They are not from the Academy," Laily noticed.

"Good," Rel said. "It means the Great One is safe."

Taking a turn to a vast corridor, they passed by the paintings and mirrors adorned in rich golden frames. The soft carpet muffled their steps. Rize looked down and regretted it instantly. The floor was smeared in blood as if someone had crawled over it. They found the body soon after.

"Dead," Angie whispered, checking the guard's pulse.

Amethyst came up closer and sniffed the severed hand that lay by the corpse. "He's been here for a while."

"And screamed for help, no doubt," Rize muttered, seeing the guard's crooked face. "His own people left him to die."

"That man knew the risks of working here." Angie tried to comfort her. "He gave his life to protect the Great One."

Balling her fists, Rize turned away. The gallery full of miraculous pictures hardly fit the ambience, but she chose to examine them instead of the corpse. She followed her team mindlessly, distracted by the landscapes she had never seen.

Rel stopped by heavy, tall doors. Their look proved with all their appearance that nothing amusing ever happened behind them. He turned his ear, eavesdropping.

"Our ruler has a company." He tensed. Taking a deep breath, Rel entered the room without knocking.

The Great One craned over a huge desk. It was a creative mess but surely had a purpose. A dozen crumpled papers, all kinds of goblets, inkwells, pencils, and books recreated Academy Town and the Citadel. He rearranged items from one place to another and remained wholly absorbed in this process.

"I came as soon as I could," Rel said, coming up briskly. "And I bear gifts! Commander," he nodded to a grim man in the room but earned a loud scoff instead of a greeting. "Sorry to find one of your men on my way here."

The commander pursed his lips and gave a polite nod. His eyes shifted, following the Great One leaving his desk. Mannerly and modest, he approached Rel and shook his hand.

"Why the delay?" Eal whispered while his broad shoulders, covered by a richly decorated robe, hid them from prying eyes.

Shorter and smaller than the Great One, Rel remained unseen. He pointed at Bram and the man on his shoulder. Eal froze, finally noticing the whole squad behind Rel's back.

"And who is this?" Curious, Eal looked at the limp body.

"Send the commander away, and I'll tell you," Rel said playfully.

"Close the doors, and let's continue," the Great One spoke louder, returning to his desk.

Rize glanced around. It was too crowded. Servants in dark suits stood quietly, their noses up. A grey-haired man with piercing hazel eyes glared at Rel with disdain. He had four armed academicians by his side, guarding the room.

"Bring a chair for our faint guest and leave us," Rel ordered the servants and waved at the body over Bram's shoulder. "You too, Commander. It won't take long."

"With all due respect, Advisor, you can order the maids, but not me," the grey-haired man scoffed, his voice haughty. "We cannot postpone the countermeasures after what happened. We have already spent too much time waiting for you to come. Your Excellency," he addressed the Great One, "it is vital to bring the attackers to justice."

"Have you found those who are responsible, Commander?" Rel smirked.

"There was no need," he said, his chin up. "My squad was the first to arrive at the scene. We found bodies. The attackers turned out to be the Lzons."

"Like in Ponktian..." the Great One muttered, moving objects on his table.

Rize frowned and traded looks with her pet. They held their breath, listening to whatever secrets the Great One would've shared out of stress.

"Bodies? Was everyone dead?" Rel mocked, infuriating the commander. "A child could cope with the capture of such dangerous criminals. Can you tell whether they were of an upper-class or nomad mercenaries? What colour were their scales? Have you found any symbols on their armour?"

"A terrorist is a terrorist. Your love for this nation is admirable, Advisor, and I'm old enough to remember its consequences," the commander said, piecing Rel with an icy look. "Have you forgotten them…again?"

"It's not the first time we've heard about Rel's memory, is it?" Rize thought.

Amethyst nodded, worry in his eyes.

"It must be the Lzons, right?" Rel scoffed. "Though you can't freely assert that the fault lies with the underwater civilisation. The fighters by the Citadel doors were human, while the Lzon bodies could've been thrown at the sites of explosions."

"Like in Ponktian," Eal muttered again.

"The Citadel knows you have a soft spot for conspiracy. But, alas, now isn't the time for your games!" The commander turned red. "They were mercenaries, no doubt. Lzon, human, a monstrous lizard – these are details of no importance."

"Enough!" the Great One cut them off. "Leave my office. The servants will escort you out."

For a moment, the commander struggled with himself, clearly wanting to answer. Nonetheless, he bowed tensely and headed for the exit.

"Well," the Great One said and shifted his gaze to the side. "Who is it?"

"Sara, lift his head, will you?" Rel asked.

The Great One grabbed a small oblong case from his desk and came up closer. Taking out neat glasses, he swiftly placed them on his nose.

"As you might guess," Rel uttered, "the fact he looks like my fighter saddens me a lot."

"Who sent him?" Eal asked.

"That's what I want to find out," Rel said. "He claimed he was sent from the Citadel by the ruler himself.

"No. He mentioned the *true* ruler," Sara said.

"Tomayto-tomahto." Bram shrugged.

The Great One rubbed his chin, pondering.

"You were sure I didn't send him," he said, a note of dismay in his voice. "Touching, but reckless, Rel."

"So, it's your work?" Rel chuckled.

"Shame on you." Eal said. "I'd never drag myself into something tasteless like using a shapeshifter as a minion."

"You realised he's a shapeshifter just by looking at him?" Rel asked, impressed.

"Of course." Eal took off his glasses. "What kind of the Great One am I if I cannot see right through people?"

"Your *sign* has nothing to do with it." Rel rolled his eyes.

"But I have many trinkets *because* of my sign," he said, toying with his glasses.

Rel sighed. "Can you tell me who he is?"

"I see abilities, but not his true face," Eal said, offended. "You're confusing the concepts of physiology and magical matter."

Rel ignored the remark and straightened his hood.

"If I were you, I'd check his limbs for a mark," Eal suggested.

Sara examined the shapeshifter's ankles, then harshly loosened the ropes on his arms. The man fell off the chair like a dummy but didn't wake up. Bram ripped his sleeves off, baring the man's shoulders. Sara stopped fussing and stepped back as if frightened.

Two black rings, split in half with a short vertical line, marked the shapeshifter's shoulder.

"A Dark Hundred tattoo," she whispered.

"A first-class assassin?" The Great One faked surprise. "Rel? Have you bullied an Elder again?"

"Not funny," Rel retorted. "Considering that Laily spotted a bunch of shady people near my front door, it was them who blew up the Citadel tower. Not the Lzons."

"I'm afraid you're right. It doesn't explain why they destroyed the archives, though," Eal said, passing by the shapeshifter and leaving him behind as if he was of no interest anymore.

The Great One's eyes faded, and his face turned grim. He came up to Rel and his charges. Plunging deep into his thoughts, he overlooked the people before him.

"To tell you the truth," Eal started his speech, "the commander might be right. Doesn't matter who dared to attack the Citadel and why, we must act accord—"

A swift slash rang across the room as the Great One gasped for air. He staggered and grabbed Bram's arm to find balance. A quiet titter crawled into the room, sending chills down Rize's spine. The blood gurgled in Eal's mouth. He collapsed, revealing his attacker.

The shapeshifter turned into his true form. His skin melted and bubbled, healing itself whilst transforming. He was of average height and had a boring face. Nothing in his grey look would make him attractive or worth the attention. An everyman. A face that slipped your memory the moment you turned away.

A man of the Dark Hundred.

"For the *true* Great One," he breathed out as if it was a blessing.

Without hesitation, the assassin lunged for another deadly slash, but the Geckos moved fast. Leaving Rize and Amethyst behind their backs, all of them got to work and disarmed the man in a blink of an eye.

Rel dodged the assassin's fist and gripped his neck. "Why?" he hissed.

Shackled with fear, Rize watched as the healers pulled the Great One away. Angie tried to fix him, but the wound opened again. She began to panic with each new spell that failed to work. Chour cursed and tried to undress him.

"The cut is deep," Chour grunted.

Nothing helped. The Great One began shaking in agony as his breath grew shallow and bubbly. Swiftly going through clanking bottles in his satchel, Chour grabbed a tiny one with a yellowish liquid inside. He generously poured it onto the wound, and a subtle hiss reached their ears.

"The weapon is poisoned!" Chour warned the others and poured the rest of the antidote into Eal's mouth. "Drink, dammit!"

"Why were you here?" Rel asked again. The gasps mixed with suffocated wheezes, piercing their ears. The shapeshifter's face turned red as the veins on his forehead swelled, threatening to pop. "Answer me!"

Accompanied by awful choking sounds, Laily found the poisoned blade, wrapped it in a table runner and hid it inside her bag.

"Rel, he can't breathe!" Rize shook his shoulder, trying to reason with her custodian. "You're killing him!"

It was a mistake.

Consumed by rage, Rel waved her off as if she was a nosy fly. Rize lost her footing and froze in mid-air. She flew across the room and hit the wall behind Amethyst. He hissed, but she could hear only a screeching ringing in her ears. A growing pain in her back, she tried to gasp but failed. Her tongue tasted iron.

"Argh…" Rize fought a cough. "Are you mad?"

"We need him alive, Rel," Sara yelled, keeping a distance.

"Tell us who sent you and I'll spare your life," Rel said.

The assassin replied with a hissing titter. He stopped trying to free himself and just smiled, having all the attention.

"Answer your master!" Rel said as his grip became tighter.

"The Darkness is my only master. Although I failed, there are ninety-nine of us to bring our lost daughter back to the World," he wheezed, gasping for air. "She needs you, and she'll take your bones sooner or later, child of—"

Crack.

His eyes flashing with fear, Rel dropped the breathless man and stepped back. The corpse fell with a heavy thud, its arms spread. Everyone went quiet. A snapped neck disfigured the body, and the shapeshifter's face slowly turned blue.

"For Universe's sake!" Chour shouted, his eyes wild. "Are you off your meds?"

Rel cowered back, then bent over and collapsed. Howling on his knees, he slammed the floor as if it was to blame for everything he had done.

"Did he say—" Sara whispered.

"Meds?!" Bram crossed his arms and glared at Chour, ready to smash him.

Chapter 18
THE PACT

The Geckoes watched Angie fussing over the injured. Rel fell into a speechless daze and stared at one spot as if he had lost his mind.

Rize and Amethyst observed the scene, engulfed by tense silence. No sounds. No thoughts. Only hungry emptiness was their passenger, freezing up Rize to screeching despair. Death and ash chased her again like a long-forgotten nightmare.

"I don't sense any charms, except for the wards that I've cast myself," Angie said, finishing the examination. "What was his treatment?"

"He took herbs…" the Great One croaked, "…mostly," Sighing heavily, he rested on a couch nearby while Chour performed his miracles. "I guess you're happy, young man, that I shared this information with you."

"For a good price," Chour mumbled. "Stay still, please."

"I had no idea Rel was sick," Laily muttered.

"Even I was unaware," Angie murmured, toying with a feather in her dreadlocks. "My spells don't work. Why?"

"None of the mortals can help him," Eal said. "We've tried everything. No matter or magic of this realm can fix his head. Ha-ha, ha-oh." He gasped, having another wave of pain.

"If it's not Rel's first time, we'll deal with it later," Sara said, her foot tapping the floor. "I'm concerned about the shapeshifter's words."

"He was the Dark Hundred, not just a shapeshifter," Eal said.

"Yes, and they kill silently as far as I know. This one mumbled about lost bones and daughters," Sara said. "Is it the guild moto or something?"

"The Dark Hundred isn't a guild. It's an ancient order of exiled noblemen. They used to serve the Great One called Liara Ent. These days they are nothing but trained hitmen," Crypt said. "If the assassin spoke of a lost daughter, he probably meant her. There were no other women in the order's history."

"Tell me you're kidding." Rize facepalmed, her face wet with a freshly made splash. "Ugh…Why is it *always* about her in this wretched place?!"

The Geckos traded confused looks.

"Care to elaborate?" Chour asked, baffled by her sudden outburst.

"No," she folded her arms stubbornly.

The Great One studied Rize for a moment. Their eyes met, and a strange spark mirrored in his gaze. She failed to decipher the emotion, though everything inside her shrunk.

"Liara being the lost daughter would explain why they wanted us both dead," Eal supported the idea. "Indeed, there must only be one of us if she's resurrected."

"But she's long dead, right?" Sara said, worried.

"Not entirely," the Great One uttered, and sweat covered his forehead. "I must check the archives."

"They were destroyed, Your Excellency," Angie reminded him and gently wiped off his cold sweat.

"Oh, Lady Angenia," he said, his voice weak. "What would I have done without you?"

Angie tensed her lips to hide a shy smile and cast another healing spell to ease the Great One's pain.

"We need to summon Grant," Eal said as his cheeks flashed with healthy redness. "He studied the matter and might have the papers I need."

"What is there to study?" Rize shook her head. "I've taught history. Liara died because of magic she couldn't contain. She literally dried out."

"A story the World needed to rebuild from the ash she left behind," Eal said. "Ash was Liara's signature, so to speak. Her magic could cause spectacular explosions. When she died, no body was found. She vanished, leaving nothing but a single rib. Her rib, no doubt. Though, rumour had it she had found a way to escape."

"If it's really her acolytes' doing, why do they think she's coming back now?" Rize asked. "Why does she need Rel?"

"That's exactly what I need to check," Eal said. "The old documents might hold a hint."

"Too much for one day," Rize whispered, rubbing her temple.

"No wallowing, Risotto." Bram grabbed her shoulders and shook firmly. "Alright, squad. Decide who'll drop by custodian Grant."

"I've been to his place." Amethyst looked at Rize as if waiting for her permission. She nodded. "I'll bring him."

The Great One waved his hand, creating a portal, for which he got another portion of Angie's laments.

"It won't last long. Hurry up," Eal tried to outcry the howling rift in the fabric of space.

Hesitating no more, Amethyst disappeared into the glowing portal. Rize chewed her lips, unable to relax. Her thoughts were lost in a wheezing sound of energy vortexes along with a gnawing feeling of uselessness.

"Leave the body here." Eal gestured, watching as Sara zealously dragged the dead shapeshifter to the exit. "I'll deal with him later. How is Rel?"

"Nothing works, Your Excellency," Chour said quietly, trying to bring Rel to his senses. "What kind of illness is this? It's like…he can't see or hear me."

"It's not just that, I'm afraid," Angie muttered. "His condition is more of a defensive reaction."

"From what?" Rize asked.

"I don't know." Angie shrugged. "Shock?"

"To tell you the truth," the Great One took a breath between his words, "Rel's case is complicated. I'm aware you've found out we are both honoured with the *greatness*, but few people know that Rel and I grew up together."

The Geckos stared at him, waiting for the explanation.

"Like, in the Academy?" Rize clarified.

"In a household," Eal said. "Rel has always been faster, bolder, and stronger. If not for the illness devouring him, I'd have to hide my face under the hood instead. The Elders tried to find a way to heal him. We've all tried and used different treatments, sought remedy from the best healers of all civilisations."

"If I can't find the root of his illness, then it's Rel's energy that suffers, not his physical body," Angie guessed.

Eal nodded, watching as she covered her mouth in distress.

"The loss of his sanity and independence is only a matter of time," he said quietly.

The corners of Rize's lips went down, and she held her breath to calm the storming emotions. For the first time, she pitied Rel, and the talk they'd had in the basement suddenly became a precious revelation. He expected to never grow old, rushing himself to live.

"So far, he managed to stop the condition with herbs, but he stopped taking them. Rel's never been spoiled by wisdom."

Amethyst jumped out of the portal, showing custodian Grant the way. As the southern man came in, the rift faded.

"Your Excellency," Grant bowed, formal as usual. "The papers."

"And herbs?" Eal cut him off. "Did you bring them?"

Grant patted his chest pocket, waiting for orders.

"Double the dosage."

"Is it even safe?" Rize wondered but got no reply.

While Angie read the Great One the needed pages from the archive, Rize doubted her every decision in life. Trying to calm down her trembling hands, she locked them behind her. She fought the upcoming tears and watched as Grant made a nasty smelling brew. He then opened Rel's mouth and helped him drink it.

Shutting her eyes, Rize tried to hide the storming emotions. She would never have thought that the world she dreamed of would be so dangerous and cruel. Her chest trembled in a silent cry that shook her, wanting to escape. She clenched her jaw harder, her tight lips turned pale. The room buzzed in murmur as everyone tried to heal the Great One. He enjoyed the attention even now. Weak and covered in his own blood, Eal bravely put on the mask of a basking ruler as if the crimson spot wasn't staining his lush robe, getting bigger.

Amethyst stayed by Rose and didn't check on his mistress after Grant came. Rize looked at the cats and the silence they shared scratched her from the inside. She wanted to know if they were talking. Were they discussing her?

Rize gritted her teeth, plotting how she could take him away. The corners of her lips lifted as the plan started to form up into defined steps.

What's wrong with you, idiot? she pinched her nose.

Having a breath, she brushed off an acidic feeling that swirled in her stomach. She'd never been jealous before, and the thoughts that emotion brought scared her to cold chills.

176

"What now?" Laily asked, her voice weak. "The spells and herbs are useless."

Rize could swear her eyes turned wet too.

"We wait." Grant came up to a tall cabinet and took out shot glasses. "Who's up for a drink?"

"I should be offended that you know where I stash the booze," Eal joked, and continued listening to Angie's narration.

Something squeezed Rize's throat, tensing her muscles so that swallowing hurt. Her red eyes met Rel's gaze. Blank and fixated, he remained indifferent as if his spirit had long left his body.

Quailed at what she observed, Rize waited in silence while the others drank. She feared of what she might say or do and refused to join Chour when he brought her a glass. She stayed alone, away from her pet and teammates. Strangely, it felt right.

Time played tricks against them as Rize watched the clock on the wall. Its hands moved forward but never fast enough. Calm and helpless, Rel didn't wake, so they waited while Chour fused with tipsy courage, tried to perform one of his miracles.

"He'll come back when he's ready," Laily whispered, her hand on his shoulder. "Let him fight his demons with dignity."

"Heresy," Chour hissed and shook her off, annoyed.

Rize balled her fists, her nails piercing her palms. She wanted to feel something other than fear. The pain helped while she watched Chour tying herbs into tiny fans. He gently waved each of them at Rel's nose, forcing him to smell the new medicine he came up with.

"Doesn't work," Chour grunted and threw away yet another smouldering plant.

He improvised a workspace on the floor. Muttering, cursing, setting herbs on fire, he made one fan after the other like a mad, stooped alchemist.

"Finally," he grunted the last word, spitting anger.

Tired and dishevelled, he triumphed over his herbs with a loud groan and slumped down on the floor. He closed his eyes in utter satisfaction.

"Wh-what happened?" Rel asked, his voice roughened.

"Rel?" Angie called out to him softly. Her fingers ran over his stubbled cheek. She looked like a troubled mother, caressing her weakened son. "How do you feel?"

"Awful," Rel groaned and pushed her hand away.

Her grip firm, Angie took him by his elbow and helped him to get up.

"My dear colleague," Rel said, seeing Grant. "You've joined our party! How is it?"

"It's sick," Grant muttered. "Rest while you can."

"Why is everyone so caring?" he asked.

"Maybe because it's easier than guessing what's wrong with you?" Rize said, arching her eyebrow.

The Great One chuckled, his nose buried in papers. The others traded troubled looks but didn't intervene.

"I forgot how vicious you can be," Rel said and straightened his hood, annoyed.

"You also forgot that the Great One is something like your brother," she retorted.

"No. I've ignored this fact deliberately for many years."

Rize groaned, throwing her hands in the air.

"Let's focus on something positive, *nie*?" Angie said, her voice calm.

"By the way," Rel got up, "why is no one busy at the scene? I'm sure all the interesting things had already been taken by other squads while you guys were chilling here."

"Rel, are you an idiot?" Rize snapped.

"You see, Risotto! My deviation wasn't so hard to diagnose, after all," Rel said, clearly enjoying the banter.

"That kind of mental deficiency is easy to discern, and you've never shown any signs of intellectual disability," Crypt said, talking to the wall as he always did when it came to discussions. "I'd say you're oddly positive and forgetful, but nothing more."

The Great One laughed but soon stopped, gasping in pain. He massaged his back, grimacing.

"Cut it out." Grant glared at them. "You, Rize Keer, need to learn some respect."

As to prove his anger, an explosion thundered outside, making everyone take a step back. The window trembled ominously, and screeching cracks silenced their worried words. They looked around to find the sound, and the vastest web of shattered glass split the window into myriad splinters.

"Another explosion?" Laily said, shocked. "Could it—"

"Get down!" Someone yelled, but it was too late.

Ringing silence stole a second before the clink and rumble of the windows shattering. Everyone threw up their hands to protect themselves from the deadly shards. A hot gust of air floated into the room, swaying the torn curtain in the wind. It hung for a while and then fell to the floor along with the cornice.

"Is it me, or did it get darker?" Sara whispered, frightened.

"Crypt, you would've told me if the Monokiese started an invasion and turned off the luminaries, right?' Rel smirked.

"No. The Archrectorate demotes scientists to miners for that." Crypt received a dozen glares and smirked. "You know the rules! Don't blame me. For now, I can tell it's not Monokiese work. We prefer to act smart, and this looks nothing like it."

Rize came up to the window and looked down from the tower. Glass particles chirped under her shoes. She squinted and observed the street, covering her nose against the acrid smoke. The shockwave collapsed all buildings in sight. Muffled groans. Curses. People called for help, trapped below crumbled houses, but no one came to the rescue.

"Something's happening while we're here doing nothing!" Bram gritted his teeth to hold back a surge of anger.

"I'm almost done," Eal raised his hand.

"Have you found anything?" Grant said.

"Anything new, you mean?" Eal frowned, putting the papers aside. "To resurrect Liara, a mage needs the sunken temple *and* her remains."

"Please, don't make me go there again," Rel drawled.

"You must persuade the king of the Runv civilisation to give us the blood diamond!" Eal fumed and groaned in pain.

"Unless you want me to kill him, we have no chance of getting inside the Runv treasury." Rel said, getting angry. "I've tried everything! The king won't deal with us."

"Everything?" Eal shifted his gaze to Laily and a smug grin emerged on his face.

"No." Rel shook his head. "Don't drag her into this."

"You *must* try again. We don't have time for your…Argh!" Eal clutched his stomach, groaning louder this time, as his wound opened again.

"Why can't you heal it?" Rel shouted, making Angie and Chour flinch.

"We're tired!" Angie lost her temper. "I've patched up the injured and *then* dragged both of you from the oblivion. I have no energy to fuse my spells."

"Oh, no. No-no-no-no-no. He's going to die." Laily babbled. "He's going to die, and Angie's magic doesn't work."

"I can do it." Rel pulled up his sleeves.

To their surprise, Angie squeezed between them and blocked Rel's way to the Great One.

"We are powerless." Angie scratched her tensed hand, stained with dried blood. "Even if I show you the easiest healing spell, there's no confidence you'd perform it well from the first try. You could make everything worse."

"I'm fine," Eal said, breathing heavily. "We need to prevent the ritual. Find the artifacts. Liara's Bone and the…Argh." He grimaced. "That bloody diamond!"

Rize observed the drama, still standing by the window. She glanced outside where one of the Citadel towers rested in ruins. Nowhere was safe. Nothing worked the way they wanted. She had no training in healing, but there was a way to save Rel and the Great One.

She hid her face in her hands and groaned.

"If nothing is working, I have a proposal...and you won't like it," she said, getting nervous.

For the first time in an hour, Amethyst gave Rize his attention. It took him a moment to connect the dots, and once he did, a blood-chilling hiss filled the room. Expecting a rant, Rize crossed her arms and winced when her pet would not stop acting out.

"No!" Amethyst barked, pricking his ears. "No deals with the demon!"

"We need the Dolmen," Rize protested. "I'm sure I can move all of us there."

"I'm sorry, *the* Dolmen?" Crypt stared at her.

"What's that?" Bram traded looks with him. "Is she making sense?"

His eyes cold, Rel looked back. Eal's clothes became wet, painting his robe with a new portion of blood.

"Fine. Let's go," Rel said.

"I promise he won't—" Rize blurted out, ready to argue.
"Oh…Well, that's not the answer I expected."

Chapter 19
BLOOD BOUNDARIES

The Nightmare Lands welcomed them with an eerie silence, rotten plants, and staled salty air.

"It's better than the ravine we've been to." Amethyst looked around. "Smells awful."

"We're by a marsh." Rize recognised the place. She narrowed her eyes, but no one was around. "Alright. Let's find the guardian."

The Geckos, Grant, and the Great One stepped into the wild thickets. The dreary twilight deceived their eyes, instilling a fear of shadows and birds that flapped and cried between ugly thorny bushes.

Century-old trees raised high, leaning down with their dry, leafless branches. They waved, creaked, and murmured terrible chants, passing down secret messages only they understood.

"Very funny, Koryn," Rize muttered, dodging another clawed twig that tried to grab her ankle.

They walked forward. The squeaky groans of rotten trunks, the horrid cracking of dead branches, and lingering whispers in the crowns of trees chased them until they reached the marsh.

"Did you hear that?" Amethyst glanced sideways.

"I choose to ignore these mischievous sounds," Rel said.

The fetid marsh, covered in algae and reeds, remained still like a dense green carpet. Water lilies scattered all over it, flickering with their withered flowers. Rize smirked. Even fragile petals gave that place a sinister look.

"It's rude to make a lady wait!" Rize shouted. "You lured us here, and now you're hiding? Really?"

"I like games, mortal," the demon's voice echoed across the marsh. "You found me, which means it wasn't that appalling."

"Did it say it likes games?" Rel whispered, looking at Amethyst.

"Be quiet and don't interfere," the cat muttered. "Don't even think around this *thing*."

Rel folded his arms in protest.

"Next time, come up with something trickier than grunting old willows," Rize said.

"Ha! One more word and I'll make you swim to me across this filthy water," the demon said, still hiding.

"So touchy about a humble criticism?" Rize played along.

Once dormant, the dirt and roots shifted under their feet. Indignant birds flew away, crying in the twilight. A damp, musty breeze lifted rotting foliage and whirled it wildly above their heads.

Rize squinted and covered her face. Creaking and rumbling, pot-bellied tree roots crawled out of the deepest marsh waters. They glistened eerily like hundreds of wet, sleeky arms entwining into a thick bridge. Finally, a tall grey figure emerged above them, floating in the air.

The demon smirked and approached the visitors, his foliage skirt rustling.

"Couldn't help yourself?" Rize said, her arms on her hips.

"What's the point of being the most powerful creature on this planet and avoiding the use of magic to entertain my guests?" Koryn asked, his eyes on her wry smile.

"That was..." Rize said, gesturing around the place. "...something."

The demon scowled, shifting his gaze.

"Your hooded friend thinks too loud," Koryn said, his voice cold. "He annoys me."

Rize looked over her shoulder. Rel snorted and stepped back.

"Koryn, we need help." Rize looked at him pleadingly. "The Great One—"

The demon narrowed his eyes and grabbed Rize by her jaw, roughly pulling her closer. Amethyst dropped into a defensive crouch. Ready to pounce and tear the deadly pale man apart, the cat growled like mad. Koryn smirked, amused by the scene, and the Geckos slowly reached for their weapons.

"Wait!" Rize raised her hand. "Everything's fine. He needs to see what we want."

A familiar feeling crawled under her skin. The demonic cold hand cupped her head, and a wave of shivers ran down Rize's neck. Memories of the past day rushed before her eyes. Koryn examined her mind gentler this time, slowing at moments where Rel and Eal were talking.

"Hm." Koryn's eyes flickered with sly sparkles. "Follow me."

The demon waved, lifting a round, rocky plateau from the deep. A green glow emitted from the malachite veins painted the marsh as the Dolmen rose from the water. People gasped quietly, awed by the power before them.

Wet and shiny, the stones lured them across the root bridge.

"I must admit, he has style," the Great One muttered, casting a covetous glance at the Dolmen.

The rain began drumming over the marsh and trees in a muffled rhythm. Gnarled twigs absorbed the unearthly moisture with a subtle crack. Only small scatterings of transparent raindrops reached the ground, sliding down the branches.

The demon waved again, creating a rocky throne for himself. He rustled forward, sat down, and locked his long, knotted fingers in a business-like manner. A crooked smile stuck to his face.

"What you're asking for is not in your interest, mortal. 'We need' is a rather vague phrase for a deal," Koryn said, his eyes drilling Rel. "Who will use the Dolmen? Is it you, Rize Keer, who pays to save the dying one? Or is it him? Let the one who wishes to pay cross the bridge.”

Shortly, Rel joined them on the plateau.

“What does this demonic mass want for its service?” he said, his voice flat.

Rize facepalmed.

“Could you at least *try* to be diplomatic?” she said.

“Don’t bother, mortal,” Koryn said calmly. “This creature of bones and flesh is so irritated that I sense his body vibrating out of anger. His thoughts out-scream yours and mine combined. I’ve heard enough…and *that* was the most decent name he gave me.”

Before Rize could get a word in, a fiery wave of spells bombarded the demon.

“You decided to set him on fire?” she shouted at Rel. “You *are* mad.”

The Geckos cowered as a sonorous, booming laughter came out from the blazing fire.

“Enough,” the demon drawled. He lightly stepped out of the raging flames and shook the dancing fire off his shoulder. “Your so-called Great One has plenty of time, but if that’s why you’re so edgy…” He clapped his hands.

The Geckos, Grant and Eal appeared by the Dolmen. Laily yelped, slipping away from the tongue of the flame that threatened to lick her ankle. Chour was leaning against a tree but fell back in the absence of such. He groaned, rubbing his sides, and his teammates helped him up. Everyone except Crypt reacted to the change of scenery. He stood still, his nose buried in his screen. It seemed that nothing could impress or distract the scientist.

“Marvellous! Everyone’s here. There must be witnesses when history is made.” Koryn beckoned them and he returned to his throne.

Rel followed the demon cautiously, leading people into the unknown.

"Listen to me, boy. Listen carefully," Koryn said and raised his finger, demanding attention. "You must pay for the power these stones provide. When it comes to healing...Let's say, lively energy which enters your mortal world must be given back to the Universe at once. After all, if something appears *somewhere*, it disappears from its place of origin."

"The Law of Conservation of Mass," Crypt said, still reading his screen.

"It's true for the realm of matter — your world." Koryn nodded. "For the realm of energies, the vital thing is balance."

"I don't like the sound of this…" Amethyst muttered.

"With all due respect, what are you leading up to?" The Great One asked.

"Much energy is needed to keep you alive." Koryn shrugged. "With all due respect."

"Someone has to die?!" Rel threw his hands.

Everyone, even Crypt, stared at the demon with their mouths open.

"What a vulgar term, 'die'." The demon clicked his tongue. "Use '*travel* to the realm of energies', '*swap* worlds', or other positive verbs. After all, death is only the beginning." Koryn flashed another sly grin. "And I'm talking about no one, but you, Relus. Isn't it why you desired to find me? Be brave and finish what you've started."

Rel gritted his teeth, breathing heavily.

"No way he's gonna accept this deal." Bram came to his senses first. "Over my dead body! Do you hear me?"

"The more people, the longer life will be," Koryn said, pleased. "You don't mind, do you?" he addressed the Dolmen.

Its carved glyphs glowed in response.

"What do you mean by 'use your own energy'?" the demon ranted.

The Dolmen's glyphs glowed brighter, and the stones vibrated as if annoyed.

"I can't come back! I… Are you kidding me, you wretched malachite?" Koryn tittered and waved the Dolmen off. "Shush! I shouldn't have asked you at all."

Confused, everyone looked at Rize, then back at the demon, then back at Rize.

"What?" She shrugged. "They're magic stones. They talk."

"Well, the Great One's advisor, another Great One, whoever with legs of meat and bones," Koryn looked at Rel. "If you're against sacrificing your life, we have a dozen mortal creatures here who altogether could replace you. A bit unfair, but it's your call."

"I..." Rel frowned.

"Careful with your next words," Grant drawled the warning.

"I…I don't know," Rel babbled.

"What do you mean you don't know? He's your ruler!" Angie thundered. "I pledged to serve the Great One. I'm ready to die, so he lives!"

"We all promised to serve, but there was nothing about trading our lives," Bram retorted, arms crossed. "I ain't gonna be the price for some necromantic ritual."

"Me too!" Laily sniffled. Her eyes became wet again.

"Laily!" Angie chocked in condemnation.

"What? The Great Ones changed hundreds of times!" she said. "The world still stands."

"This is wrong." Angie shook her head. "We can save him in the name of a bright future for all civilisations. Can you imagine what will happen if he's dead?"

"Lady Angenia…" Eal said, flattered. He couldn't say more, wincing in pain.

"Not everyone wants to sacrifice themselves for the sake of others." Sara spat at her feet.

"Exactly. I'm not ready to give up Rel so easily," Laily said and looked at her custodian, blushing. "If need be, I'll stop you by gnawing into your body."

"I need to think…" Rel drawled, baffled by that confession.

"Sure." Koryn scoffed, watching him pacing the plateau. "Eal has about twenty minutes left! Nothing personal, Your Excellency," he apologised.

His body weak, the Great One fainted, making everyone around him panic. Crypt stepped away and continued reading his screen.

"Meanwhile, I'll talk with a charming friend of mine. Have you brought me something to read, Rize Keer? I confess the books you left with me this morning seemed a bit dull. Here's your satchel, by the way." He took the bag out of thin air and tossed it to Rize.

"Books?" Amethyst glared at his mistress. "Now it's clear to which *book club* you went once a week!"

Rize stooped under his gaze and giggled nervously. "Everything happened so quickly today," Rize said, her voice trembled. "I didn't think of a book for you and—" she noticed someone in the corner of her eye.

His steps cautious, Crypt slowly approached the demon. He propped his glasses, avoiding rushed moves, and held out his screen to the demon.

"Well, hello, mortal..." Koryn cooed. He looked at Rize curiously, then back at wide-eyed Crypt, then at the object in his hand. "What are you giving me? Rize Keer, does *it* speak?" he tilted his head, examining the scientist. "If necessary, I can heal that one too for a small fee."

"Read," Crypt squeezed out a word and offered his screen persistently. "You can read it."

"It speaks! I can read, yes." The demon nodded, taking the device. "Thank you. Now go back to your place. Come on, come on…Sit on the rock where you sat." He chuckled. "What a strange boy. I don't understand even half of his thoughts."

Crypt returned to his place and took out another screen, identical to his first one. Distracted from the Great One, the Geckos witnessed the scene in confusion as if wondering how two screens could fit in his armour. Crypt cleared his throat and began reading again.

Rize smiled but stopped once she noticed the judgmental faces of those around her.

"I'll show you how to use it," she said, and stepped towards Koryn, deftly dodging Amethyst's bite.

Walking back and forth, Rel watched what happened from the distance. He saw Rize chatting merrily with the demon and shook his head. Suddenly he stopped as if charmed.

"Have you made your decision, mortal?" Koryn noticed his hesitation.

"I might have," he said, staring at the Dolmen and its glowing glyphs.

Grant left his post by the Great One and traded looks with Rel. He moved forward carefully when the demon caught his cautious glance.

"I can't decide whether you're retarded or stupid," the demon addressed the custodians.

"Why? What's going on?" Rize said, worried.

"They want to free me, I think." Koryn chuckled and turned to the Dolmen. "Is this the fault of your stony hands?"

The stones glowed again in response.

"Oh?" Koryn shifted his body and turned back to the men. "*That's* an option that might work, actually…"

The demon looked over the crowd before him and pinched his nose, tired.

"Did this empty-headed gem mention to you the risks of the pact with me?" the demon asked, baring his sharp teeth in a chilling grin. "You might die if your motives are dishonest. Just like that." He snapped his fingers. "Without the higher goal of saving your friend there."

"It didn't," Rel replied, his eyes darkened.

"How nice we could figure everything out in advance!" Koryn dramatized, clapping. "I'll tell you a secret. I don't care whether you die, you *and* your so-called Great One, or only he alone. Existence in this world is absurd! If I had it my way, I would've died long ago in mere protest."

"I'll take my chances anyway," Rel said and smirked. "Heal the Great One."

"Which one?" the demon tilted his head.

"Not. Me," Rel greeted through his teeth.

"No!" Laily pushed him angrily while others supported her mood by shouting curses. "You are not in your mind if you want to trade your spirit—"

"No-no, my sweet girl. He'll share one tiny artefact with me," the demon corrected her. "His spirit is a bit strong for my acidic stomach."

"I promise to bring you the blood and release you of this vessel," Rel brought them back to the subject.

"And use my demonic energy as a payment to travel to the sunken temple," Koryn continued his thought for him. "You'll have my gratitude if you succeed. I'm sick of this place."

Koryn winked at Rize as the Dolmen glowed brighter than ever. Once again, she noticed Rel trade looks with Grant and something clenched her heart inside.

Only the blood that had summoned a demon can set him free. Rize thought. *If it works, then it means...* She forgot how to breathe. *Rel has Liara's blood.*

Watching Rize, the demon tittered, clearly aware of her thoughts. Their eyes met. Finally, he sighed after a longing moment of silence.

"No, mortal," Koryn said. "It would be a true gift if he was her son. Although," he leaned forward in his seat, "the hooded boy doesn't share Liara's bloodline, he knows where to get enough of it to separate me from the Dolmen. Oh, you are *something*, Relus! Plan all this? Just to meet me?"

"I don't understand," Rize mumbled as fear shackled her thinking. "What is he talking about? Rel?!"

The demon pierced the hooded man with his glossy black eyes. "Are you willing to make a pact?"

Rel ignored all the voices screaming at him. "Yes," he said.

"I need a guarantee you'll come back," Koryn cooed.

Rel stepped forward fearfully, seeing the enthusiasm in the demon's eyes. The Geckos tried to drag him away from the Dolmen. He didn't budge. Instead, he waved off his charges and a gust of wind pushed them back.

Waking up in a fever, the Great One tried to stop Rel, but failed. He was too weak. Angie helped him to stand but refused to bring him closer to the demon.

"Tick-tock." Koryn hurried them, enjoying the drama.

"I'll bring you a drop of Liara's blood when I have the blood diamond," Rel swore. "I'll release you from your service."

"You are not a trustworthy subject at all," Koryn continued bargaining. "Leave me something!"

"Like?" Rel said.

The demon's face brightened. A crooked smile appeared on his face again as his eyes sent naughty gleams.

"Give me her bone," Koryn demanded.

Chapter 20
WHAT GOES AROUND COMES AROUND

"The Bone was stolen," Rel retorted. "I don't have it."

"Oh, but you do," Koryn murmured. "I feel it in you."

A troubled mutter raised above the Geckos. Grant frowned and shielded the Great One who looked paler than before. Nonetheless, he tried to stand upright and looked at Rel in disbelief.

The Dolmen gleamed brighter as if talking to its guardian. Koryn nodded, listening to the knowledge it shared, and with every new flash, his grin became wider.

"Could it be…" Koryn slowly shifted his gaze to Rel, "…that you don't remember your visions, Dreamcatcher?"

"What—" Eal panted in fever. "Rel?"

Koryn touched the Dolmen and drew out a ball of energy, blinding those who stood too close. The sphere gleamed a green light and spread waves of warmth across the plateau.

"I'll trade this to heal your ruler, your sick head, and open a portal to the Runv civilisation," Koryn said his final offer. "Instead, I'll take the Bone from you until you bring me Liara's blood."

He floated towards Rel and whispered the words in a long-forgotten language to his ear.

As if the world was against the conjuring, the trees around them creaked angrily under the risen wind. Moving faster than a human eye could see, Koryn dived his demonic hand into Rel's chest.

Rel gasped in pain, but no one dared to help his escape.

"Hm, sorry," the demon frowned. "It's a bit lower."

The next moment Koryn ripped out a dangerously glowing bone right from Rel's stomach with a ringing crack. A quiet, victorious laugh echoed across the plateau. Everyone could see now a perfectly intact ancient rib.

194

The Great One mumbled rich curses, refusing to accept the truth.

"You had it?" Eal said. "This whole time. You had it. How? Why did you take it?"

"I didn't!" Rel protested. "It was a dream. I…How could I possibly—"

"Easy, easy," Koryn hushed them. "Business first. Do you accept the pact?" he said, holding the Bone in one hand and the ball of energy in the other.

"I do." His eyes up, Rel clenched his jaw.

Eal breathed unevenly and leaned to Grant when the demon floated closer. Still covered in his own blood, the Great One courageously looked into the demonic eyes and their alluring darkness. Amused, Koryn joined his hands and sent the lively energy between two men.

The pulsating surges of warmth spread where their bodies hurt. When the magic dissolved into their flesh, the weather calmed down and the birds started crying again.

"It is done," Koryn said, dusting his hands. "Energy must saturate your bodies soon enough. Give it time."

"What will happen now?" Rize asked, struggling to accept what she had just witnessed.

"I'll use the stones," Rel said, his eyes flashed hungrily.

Bram grabbed him from behind.

"Wait a minute," he said. "Why the rush?"

Angie joined him, nervous. "Rel, we must think this through. I don't like anything that's happening."

Rel ignored them. He fixated on the Dolmen, and it seemed nothing in the world mattered to him anymore.

Rize widened her eyes.

I led him here… she thought. *He set the whole thing up. That's why he was so eager to come.*

"You finally got it," Koryn said, full of surprise.

"You lying bastard!" Rize glared at Rel. "It was never about saving me, was it? You knew! You dreamt of me coming here!"

"It's not a good time, Risotto." Rel passed by, but she kicked him, looking for a fight.

"Wow! Easy, girl!" Chour tried to hold Rize back but got a slap to his cheek. "Argh! What the demon is going on with you two?"

"Ask him!" she snapped. "He set everything up!"

"This accusation is delusional," Rel scoffed.

"As delusional as it is to think that you could get the remains of the most dangerous woman in history whilst sleeping," she said. "Or find a girl who would believe a seer and find the Dolmen that you desperately need?"

"What?" Sara chuckled shortly.

"He is the key to Liara's resurrection," Rize said, getting angrier. "That's why the assassin came for me and Amethyst. The Dark Hundred knew I could lead them to the Dolmen!"

Amethyst gaped at Rose, clearly starting a telepathic conversation. Their tails swept the plateau.

"You lied to me," Rize whispered, shaking with anger. Her hands itched. She rubbed her fingers and they squeaked quietly, her skin dry. "You used me! Why? To stop the resurrection? To heal yourself?"

"He wants the Source," the demon said light-heartedly.

"By the Source, you mean…like the one from the legend?" Sara said, baffled. It seemed she lost the ability to think straight. "It's not real, right?"

Grant and Rel lowered their gaze. Nothing they could say would calm everyone down.

"You knew I'd lead you to the Dolmen from the beginning. That's why you clung to me in Ponktian. That's why you cared so much for my transfer and accepted me into the squad, even though I could go back any minute!" Rize gulped a suffocating lump. Her throat was sore from yelling. "You made me believe I found my place."

Laily whistled, amazed.

"No person in the whole world can claim Relus has never deceived them. I'll help you forget." Koryn stroked Rize's shoulder, feeding upon her raging emotions.

"Take your hands off my people, demon." Rel pushed Koryn as his grey fingers drew out her energy.

"I see only one demon here, and he wears a hood." Weakened, Rize pierced her custodian with a cold stare. "I don't want to be anywhere near you. Finish your business and send us home."

"What?" Amethyst said, his eyes confused. He looked at Rose by his side, and suddenly she butted him as if encouraging. "I...I don't want to come back."

"Pardon?" Rize stared at him in disbelief.

"I'm *not* going," the cat said louder, lowering his head.

A forced scoff escaped Rize's chest as she cowered her head, processing his words. Her eyes darted while the rest of the squad witnessed the unravelling scene.

"Have you heard what I said?" she asked, her voice trembling. "What he did?" she shrieked.

"Rize..." Ashamed, the cat stepped back, increasing the distance between them. "Calm down."

"I can't believe you're—" She cut off herself, finally getting where this was going.

The corners of her lips went down, trembling. She blinked more often to prevent the tears from running down her checks.

"What will *I* do in Ponktian? Huh? Have you thought about that?" Amethyst said. "I finally have a *life* here! Friends and…dreams, for Universe's sake!"

"No," Rize whispered, shaking her head. She sniffled. Her nose red, she turned into mess. "No. You're not doing this to me."

They drilled each other with cold stares until Amethyst backed off.

He looked away, his moves awkward. "You said you loved me," he muttered.

The claws of betrayal slashed Rize again, and a stressed giggle rang across the plateau.

"Let me go," Amethyst whispered. "Please."

She shook her head like a child, her cloud-white hair trembling.

"Please, Rize. Let me go," he pleaded.

A stiff yelp. Both of her hands lifted slowly as Rize covered her mouth. They were dry. It distracted her for a moment, though her heart ached as if bleeding. She turned them around and chuckled.

"It wasn't love, Angie," she looked at the healer, defeated. "Betrayal shaped my spirit's final form." She sniffled and sighed, her breath uneven.

"Little Flower," she uttered, a crease on her forehead. "Oh…"

Finally, Rize looked at Rel, her head high and proud.

"There was no Dedication ceremony for me. I'm not *yours*," she spat. "I'm going home."

Rel watched her stooped figure walk away. The squad plunged into a disturbing murmur. Sara reached Rize but stopped halfway.

"Shut it and stay where you stand. All of you!" Rel barked. "That's an order!"

They obeyed and spoke no more, their faces grim. The demon smirked, seeing Rel's heavy breathing and wandering eyes.

"Pathetic attempt to catch a stormy wind in a jar," Koryn said, his mood up. "It was a long-lasting gamble for you, boys." His glance jumped from Grant, then to Eal, and then back to Rel. "Forget about your pups for a moment and indulge me. Your bet was correct. Rize Keer brought you to the stones, but it's just a starting point. You *do* realise the Dolmen is a portal, not the Source itself, don't you?" His pale lips quivered in a mocking smile.

Rel blinked, lost in the question like a silly child.

"Oh," the demon was surprised. "Ha. Ha-ha-ha. Liara enchanted the Dolmen as a portal to the temple that rests in the waters of the Lzon civilisation."

"If that's so — fine. Now open the portal to Runv," Rel said. "When I have the blood, I'll find the Source with or without your help, to stop Liara's resurrection."

Rize snorted, rolling her eyes.

"How serious," Koryn said and pursed his lips. "Don't forget to set me free before that."

The demon waved his wrist, bending fingers. A current of air formed a blade that hacked his skin swiftly. The demonic canker splattered onto the stones.

Smeared in otherworldly matter, the Dolmen flashed again. An invisible wave knocked all living creatures to the ground, opening the portal summoned by the demonic pact.

Ears ringing, Rize opened her eyes. She gasped in an agony of skull-cracking pain. The Geckos shivered on the ground, groaning and screaming while Rel stood straight under the raging wild magic of the malachite veins.

"Koryn?" Rize rolled over and got to her knees. She yelped, seeing her fingers crumbling into glowing particles. "What's happening?" She stared at her hands and turned them around.

"Follow the current, mortal! And let it guide you well!" The demon roared in laughter, slapping the plateau as if playing the drums. "I love dark pacts! Do you feel the stormy energy coming through your body?"

The force seemed unbearable indeed. Rize fell on her belly, her eyes shut. She shivered as glowing particles spread across her chest and waist. A suppressed groan slipped from her trembling lips, and a chunk of her hip dissolved into nothingness.

"He lied to me," she whispered, suffocating in tears.

"Mortals are deceitful. The question is what you'll do about it when you wake up," the demon said. "Don't fight the river you can't control. Swim in it."

"Koryn," she called him out, fighting the void of unconsciousness.

"Yes?"

"I must say, I like you more than my people," Rize muttered. "Mortals and demons are not so different."

Feeling the deadly cold palm and gnarled fingers on her cheek, Rize drowned in a troubled sleep while her body dissolved into a myriad of particles and then disappeared.

THE END OF BOOK TWO
of
RIZE KEER SERIES

RIZE KEER

FEAR THE HERALD

L.M. FILI

As hermits refuse the company of men,
So should you fight the sweet call of brass trumpets.
Loud and clear, they summon fame upon the weak
Whilst flatter cracks their pious spirits.

— An old Lzon teaching.

<u>Corrupting the best of us makes the worst reign.</u>

What would you do if fame and flattery made you sacrifice everything you have? Your true self? Your friend? Your beloved?

Naive loyalty has led Rize Keer to a place where freedom has no value, and trust poisons better than any toxin. The underground Runv civilisation welcomes her along with the Geckos to start a dangerous quest to prevent a necromantic ritual and save the world as she knows it.

As *the Abovers*, the Geckos become celebrities, even though they serve the Great One – the man behind all troubles in the underground and underwater realms, as they say. Having lost her faith in the Citadel order, Rize explores the independent civilisations – Runv and Lzon – from a new perspective.

No matter what calling she decides to follow, brass trumpets will praise the weak to pave a way for the sly. How would she act, trapped in a jewelled cage of royal family, when a single word of reason could lead to a riot or slaughter?

This is the final book in Rize's personal journey.

RIZE KEER

FIGHTING THE CURRENT

BOOK 2 IN THE SERIES

L.M. FILI

<u>Share Your Thoughts With Others</u>!

Did you enjoy Rize Keer? It would mean so much to me if you wrote a review of my novel and its characters on Amazon or Goodreads. Your feedback will help me improve my writing for future projects AND support me as an independent creator. Let's make Rize Keer better together!

Thanks in advance for your help. You're awesome!

About the author

I created a universe where I could reflect on the world's bustle. I'm a sociable hermit. Sounds confusing, but I detest being an open book. Therefore, you will know only the side of me that I allow you to see.

After all, you are here because of the book and not because of my personality. If you fell in love with Rize and Amethyst, I invite you to travel across their world with me. If you'd like to stay updated with the latest stories, you can find me online. Feel free to contact me if you have questions or thoughts to share. I'm more than happy to chat.

My dirty secrets are…

- o I hate reading because of my dyslexia, but I'm adult enough to realise that nothing in this world is straightforward except ignorance.
- o Exploring the new is my engine in life. I enjoy talking about philosophy or the nature of human existence.
- o Lady Gray tea is the best tea in the world. I'm open to debate.
- o I'm a hugger, though my face implies the opposite.

<u>Keep in touch via:</u>
e-mail: fili.author@gmail.com

<u>Acknowledgements</u>

I want to thank everyone for their life energy. I believe that we are all connected and serve as mirrors of each other's lives. We reflect each other's souls and trigger egos.

You are the best teachers on this planet.

Thanks to my readers. Because of you, I'm not giving up.
Thanks to the authors, who refused to leave me in trouble.

Special thanks to Jason Malone for his love for words, history, and writing. Your editing and tutoring made this book happen.